The Short Story Series

GENERAL EDITOR   JAMES GIBSON

ADVENTURE
ANIMAL
DETECTION
HORROR
HUMOUR
LOVE
SCIENCE FICTION
SEA
SPORT
SUPERNATURAL
TRAVEL
WESTERN

The Short Story Series

Travel

CHOSEN BY

Edward Leeson

John Murray

Albemarle Street London

Printed and bound in Great Britain
by Butler & Tanner Ltd,
Frome and London

0 7195 3666 9

CONTENTS

Miss Bracegirdle Does Her Duty
by Stacy Aumonier   1
The Story-Teller by Saki   16
An Elaborate Elopement by W. W. Jacobs   21
Under the Deck-Awnings by Jack London   29
The Better Part of Valour by Celia Dale   36
The Long-Distance Train by W. B. Maxwell   50
Miss Winchelsea's Heart by H. G. Wells   65
Enemies by Nadine Gordimer   81
The Rough Crossing by F. Scott Fitzgerald   90
A lesson in Crime by G. D. H. and M. Cole   108
Acknowledgements   120

Stacy Aumonier

Miss Bracegirdle Does Her Duty

'This is the room, madame.'

'Ah, thank you ... thank you.'

'Does it appear satisfactory to madame?'

'Oh, yes, thank you ... quite.'

'Does madame require anything further?'

'Er—if not too late, may I have a hot bath?'

'*Parfaitement*, madame. The bathroom is at the end of the passage on the left. I will go and prepare it for madame.'

'There is one thing more.... I have had a very long journey. I am very tired. Will you please see that I am not disturbed in the morning until I ring.'

'Certainly, madame.'

Millicent Bracegirdle was speaking the truth—she *was* tired. In the sleepy cathedral town of Easingstoke, from which she came, it was customary for everyone to speak the truth. It was customary, moreover, for everyone to lead simple, self-denying lives—to give up their time to good works and elevating thoughts. One had only to glance at little Miss Bracegirdle to see that in her were epitomized all the virtues and ideals of Easingstoke. Indeed, it was the pursuit of duty which had brought her to the Hôtel de l'Ouest at Bordeaux on this summer's night. She had travelled from Easingstoke to London, then without a break to Dover, crossed that horrid stretch of sea to Calais, entrained for Paris, where she of necessity had to spend four hours—a terrifying experience—and then had come on to Bordeaux, arriving at midnight. The reason of this journey being that someone had to come to Bordeaux to meet her young sister-in-law, who was arriving the next day from South America. The sister-in-law was married to a missionary in Paraguay, but the climate not agreeing with her, she was returning to England. Her dear brother, the dean, would have come himself, but the claims on his time were so extensive, the parishioners would miss him so ... it was clearly Millicent's duty to go.

She had never been out of England before, and she had a horror of travel, and an ingrained distrust of foreigners. She spoke a little

French—sufficient for the purposes of travel and for obtaining any modest necessities, but not sufficient for carrying on any kind of conversation. She did not deplore this latter fact, for she was of the opinion that French people were not the kind of people that one would naturally want to have conversation with; broadly speaking, they were not quite 'nice', in spite of their ingratiating manners.

The dear dean had given her endless advice, warning her earnestly not to enter into conversation with strangers, to obtain all information from the police, railway officials—in fact, any one in an official uniform. He deeply regretted to say that he was afraid that France was not a country for a woman to travel about in *alone*. There were loose, bad people about, always on the look-out. . . . He really thought perhaps he ought not to let her go. It was only by the utmost persuasion, in which she rather exaggerated her knowledge of the French language and character, her courage, and indifference to discomfort, that she managed to carry the day.

She unpacked her valise, placed her things about the room, tried to thrust back the little stabs of homesickness as she visualized her darling room at the deanery. How strange and hard and unfriendly seemed these foreign hotel bedrooms—heavy and depressing, no chintz and lavender and photographs of . . . all the dear family, the dean, the nephews and nieces, the interior of the cathedral during harvest festival, no samplers and needlework or coloured reproductions of the paintings by Marcus Stone. Oh dear, how foolish she was! What did she expect?

She disrobed and donned a dressing-gown; then, armed with a sponge-bag and towel, she crept timidly down the passage to the bathroom, after closing her bedroom door and turning out the light. The gay bathroom cheered her. She wallowed luxuriously in the hot water, regarding her slim legs with quiet satisfaction. And for the first time since leaving home there came to her a pleasant moment—a sense of enjoyment in her adventure. After all, it *was* rather an adventure, and her life had been peculiarly devoid of it. What queer lives some people must live, travelling about, having experiences! How old was she? Not really old—not by any means. Forty-two? Forty-three? She had shut herself up so. She hardly ever regarded the potentialities of age. As the world went, she was a well-preserved woman for her age. A life of self-abnegation, simple living, healthy walking and fresh air, had kept her younger than these hurrying, pampered city people.

Love? yes, once when she was a young girl . . . he was a schoolmaster, a most estimable kind gentleman. They were never engaged—not actually, but it was a kind of understood thing. For three years it went on, this pleasant understanding and friendship. He was so gentle, so distinguished and considerate. She would have been happy to have continued in this strain for ever. But there was something lacking. Stephen had curious restless lapses. From the physical aspect of marriage she shrunk—yes, even with Stephen, who was gentleness and kindness itself. And then one day ... one day he went away—vanished, and never returned. They told her he had married one of the country girls—a girl who used to work in Mrs Forbes's dairy—not a very nice girl, she feared, one of these fast, pretty, foolish women. Heigho! well, she had lived that down, destructive as the blow appeared at the time. One lives everything down in time. There is always work, living for others, faith, duty. ... At the same time she could sympathize with people who found satisfaction in unusual experiences.

There would be lots to tell the dear dean when she wrote to him on the morrow: nearly losing her spectacles on the restaurant car; the amusing remarks of an American child on the train to Paris; the curious food everywhere, nothing simple and plain; the two English ladies at the hotel in Paris who told her about the death of their uncle—the poor man being taken ill on Friday and dying on Sunday afternoon, just before tea-time; the kindness of the hotel proprietor who had sat up for her; the prettiness of the chambermaid. Oh, yes, everyone was really very kind. The French people, after all, were very nice. She had seen nothing—nothing but was quite nice and decorous. There would be lots to tell the dean tomorrow.

Her body glowed with the friction of the towel. She again donned her night attire and her thick, woollen dressing-gown. She tidied up the bathroom carefully in exactly the same way she was accustomed to do at home, then once more gripping her sponge-bag and towel, and turning out the light, she crept down the passage to her room. Entering the room she switched on the light and shut the door quickly. Then one of those ridiculous things happened— just the kind of thing you would expect to happen in a foreign hotel. The handle of the door came off in her hand.

She ejaculated a quiet 'Bother!' and sought to replace it with one hand, the other being occupied with the towel and sponge-bag. In doing this she behaved foolishly, for thrusting the knob carelessly against the steel pin—without properly securing it—she only succeeded in pushing the pin farther into the door and the knob was not adjusted. She uttered another little 'Bother!' and put her sponge-bag and towel down on the floor. She then tried to recover the pin with her left hand, but it had gone in too far.

'How very foolish!' she thought. 'I shall have to ring for the chambermaid—and perhaps the poor girl has gone to bed.'

She turned and faced the room, and suddenly the awful horror was upon her. *There was a man asleep in her bed!*

The sight of that swarthy face on the pillow, with its black tousled hair and heavy moustache, produced in her the most terrible moment of her life. Her heart nearly stopped. For some seconds she could neither think nor scream, and her first thought was: 'I mustn't scream!'

She stood there like one paralysed, staring at the man's head and the great curved hunch of his body under the clothes. When she began to think she thought very quickly, and all her thoughts worked together. The first vivid realization was that it wasn't the man's fault; it was *her* fault. *She was in the wrong room.* It was the man's room. The rooms were identical, but there were all his things about, his clothes thrown carelessly over chairs, his collar and tie on the wardrobe, his great heavy boots and the strange yellow trunk. She must get out somehow, anyhow.

She clutched once more at the door, feverishly driving her finger-nails into the hole where the elusive pin had vanished. She tried to force her fingers in the crack and open the door that way, but it was of no avail. She was to all intents and purposes locked in— locked in a bedroom in a strange hotel alone with a man ... a foreigner ... *a Frenchman*! She must think. She must think. ... She switched off the light. If the light was off he might not wake up. It might give her time to think how to act. It was surprising that he had not awakened. If he *did* wake up, what would he do? How could she explain herself? He wouldn't believe her. No one would believe her. In an English hotel it would be difficult enough, but here where she wasn't known, where they were all foreigners and consequently antagonistic ... merciful heavens!

She *must* get out. Should she wake the man? No, she couldn't do that. He might murder her. He might ... Oh, it was too awful to contemplate! Should she scream? ring for the chambermaid? But no, it would be the same thing. People would come rushing. They would find her there in the strange man's bedroom after mid-night—she, Millicent Bracegirdle, sister of the Dean of Easing-stoke! Easingstoke!

Visions of Easingstoke flashed through her alarmed mind.

Visions of the news arriving, women whispering around tea-tables: 'Have you heard, my dear?... Really no one would have imagined! Her poor brother! He will of course have to resign, you know, my dear. Have a little more cream, my love.'

Would they put her in prison? She might be in the room for the purpose of stealing or ... She might be in the room for the purpose of breaking every one of the ten commandments. There was no explaining it away. She was a ruined woman, suddenly and irretrievably, unless she could open the door. The chimney? Should she climb up the chimney? But where would that lead to? And then she visualized the man pulling her down by her legs when she was already smothered in soot. Any moment he might wake up. . . .

She thought she heard the chambermaid going along the passage. If she had wanted to scream, she ought to have screamed before. The maid would know she had left the bathroom some minutes ago. Was she going to her room? Suddenly she remembered that she had told the chambermaid that she was not to be disturbed until she rang the next morning. That was something. Nobody would be going to her room to find out that she was not there.

An abrupt and desperate plan formed in her mind. It was already getting on for one o'clock. The man was probably a quite harmless commercial traveller or businessman. He would probably get up about seven or eight o'clock, dress quickly, and go out. She would hide under his bed until he went. Only a matter of a few hours. Men don't look under their beds, although she made a religious practice of doing so herself. When he went he would be sure to open the door all right. The handle would be lying on the floor as though it had dropped off in the night. He would probably ring for the chambermaid or open it with a penknife. Men were so clever at those things. When he had gone she would creep out and steal back to her room, and then there would be no necessity to give any explanation to anyone. But heavens! What an experience! Once under the white frill of that bed she would be safe till the morning. In daylight nothing seemed so terrifying.

With feline precaution she went down on her hands and knees and crept toward the bed. What a lucky thing there was that broad white frill! She lifted it at the foot of the bed and crept under. There was just sufficient depth to take her slim body. The floor was fortunately carpeted all over, but it seemed very close and dusty. Suppose she coughed or sneezed! Anything might happen.

Of course ... it would be much more difficult to explain her presence under the bed than to explain her presence just inside the door. She held her breath in suspense. No sound came from above, but under this frill it was difficult to hear anything. It was almost more nerve-racking than hearing everything ... listening for signs and portents. This temporary escape in any case would give her time to regard the predicament detachedly. Up to the present she had not been able to visualize the full significance of her action. She had in truth lost her head. She had been like a wild animal, consumed with the sole idea of escape ... a mouse or a cat would do this kind of thing—take cover and lie low. If only it hadn't all happened *abroad*! She tried to frame sentences of explanation in French, but French escaped her. And then—they talked so rapidly, these people. They didn't listen. The situation was intolerable. Would she be able to endure a night of it?

At present she was not altogether uncomfortable, only stuffy and ... very, very frightened. But she had to face six or seven or eight hours of it—perhaps even then discovery in the end! The minutes flashed by as she turned the matter over and over in her head. There was no solution. She began to wish she had screamed or awakened the man. She saw now that that would have been the wisest and most politic thing to do; but she had allowed ten minutes or a quarter of an hour to elapse from the moment when the chambermaid would know that she had left the bathroom. They would want an explanation of what she had been doing in the man's bedroom all that time. Why hadn't she screamed before?

She lifted the frill an inch or two and listened. She thought she heard the man breathing but she couldn't be sure. In any case it gave her more air. She became a little bolder, and thrust her face partly through the frill so that she could breathe freely. She tried to steady her nerves by concentrating on the fact that—well, there it was. She had done it. She must make the best of it. Perhaps it would be all right after all.

'Of course I shan't sleep,' she kept on thinking. 'I shan't be able to. In any case it will be safer not to sleep. I must be on the watch.'

She set her teeth and waited grimly. Now that she had made up her mind to see the thing through in this manner she felt a little calmer. She almost smiled as she reflected that there would certainly be something to tell the dear dean when she wrote to him tomorrow. How would he take it? Of course he would believe it—he had never doubted a single word that she had uttered in her life—but the story would sound so ... preposterous. In Easingstoke it would be almost impossible to envisage such an experience. She, Millicent Bracegirdle, spending a night under a strange man's bed in a foreign hotel! What would those women think? Fanny Shields and that garrulous old Mrs Rushbridger? Perhaps ... yes, perhaps it would be advisable to tell the dear dean to let the story go no further. One could hardly expect Mrs Rushbridger to ... not make implications ... exaggerate.

Oh, dear! What were they all doing now? They would be all asleep, everyone in Easingstoke. Her dear brother always retired at ten-fifteen. He would be sleeping calmly and placidly, the sleep of the just ... breathing the clear sweet air of Sussex, not this—oh, it *was* stuffy! She felt a great desire to cough. She mustn't do that. Yes, at nine-thirty all the servants summoned to the library—a short service—never more than fifteen minutes, her brother didn't believe in a great deal of ritual—then at ten o'clock cocoa for everyone. At ten-fifteen bed for everyone. The dear sweet bedroom with the narrow white bed, by the side of which she had knelt every night as long as she could remember—even in her dear mother's day—and said her prayers.

Prayers! Yes, that was a curious thing. This was the first night in her life's experience that she had not said her prayers on retiring. The situation was certainly very peculiar ... exceptional, one might call it. God would understand and forgive such a lapse. And yet after all, why ... what was to prevent her saying her prayers? Of course she couldn't kneel in the proper devotional attitude, that would be a physical impossibility; nevertheless, perhaps her prayers might be just as efficacious ... if they came from the heart. So little Miss Bracegirdle curved her body and placed her hands in a devout attitude in front of her face and quite inaudibly murmured her prayers under the strange man's bed.

'Our Father which art in heaven, Hallowed be Thy name. Thy kingdom come. Thy will be done in earth as it is in heaven. Give us this day our daily bread. And forgive us our trespasses. ...'

Trespasses! Yes, surely she was trespassing on this occasion, but God would understand. She had not wanted to trespass. She was an unwitting sinner. Without uttering a sound she went through her usual prayers in her heart. At the end she added fervently:

'Please God protect me from the dangers and perils of this night.'

Then she lay silent and inert, strangely soothed by the effort of praying. 'After all,' she thought, 'it isn't the attitude which matters—it is that which occurs deep down in us.'

For the first time she began to meditate—almost to question—

church forms and dogma. If an attitude was not indispensable, why a building, a ritual, a church at all? Of course her dear brother couldn't be wrong, the church was so old, so very old, its root deep buried in the story of human life, it was only that . . . well, outward forms *could* be misleading. Her own present position for instance. In the eyes of the world she had, by one silly careless little action, convicted herself of being the breaker of every single one of the ten commandments.

She tried to think of one of which she could not be accused. But no—even to dishonouring her father and mother, bearing false witness, stealing, coveting her neighbour's . . . husband! That was the worst thing of all. Poor man! He might be a very pleasant honourable married gentleman with children and she—she was in a position to compromise him! Why hadn't she screamed? Too late! Too late!

It began to get very uncomfortable, stuffy, but at the same time draughty, and the floor was getting harder every minute. She changed her position stealthily and controlled her desire to cough. Her heart was beating rapidly. Over and over again recurred the vivid impression of every little incident and argument that had occurred to her from the moment she left the bathroom. This must, of course, be the room next to her own. So confusing, with perhaps twenty bedrooms all exactly alike on one side of a passage—how was one to remember whether one's number was 115 or 116?

Her mind began to wander idly off into her schooldays. She was always very bad at figures. She disliked Euclid and all those subjects about angles and equations—so unimportant, not leading anywhere. History she liked, and botany, and reading about strange foreign lands, although she had always been too timid to visit them. And the lives of great people, *most* fascinating—Oliver Cromwell, Lord Beaconsfield, Lincoln, Grace Darling—*there* was a heroine for you—General Booth, a great, good man, even if a little vulgar. She remembered dear old Miss Trimming talking about him one afternoon at the vicar of St Bride's garden party. She was *so* amusing. She . . . *Good heavens!*

Almost unwittingly, Millicent Bracegirdle had emitted a violent sneeze!

It was finished! For the second time that night she was conscious of her heart nearly stopping. For the second time that night she was so paralysed with fear that her mentality went to pieces. Now she would hear the man get out of bed. He would walk across to the door, switch on the light, and then lift up the frill. She could almost see that fierce moustached face glaring at her and growling something in French. Then he would thrust out an arm and drag her out. And then? O God in heaven! What then? . . .

'I shall scream before he does it. Perhaps I had better scream now. If he drags me out he will clap his hand over my mouth. Perhaps chloroform. . . .'

But somehow she could not scream. She was too frightened even for that. She lifted the frill and listened. Was he moving stealthily across the carpet? She thought—no, she couldn't be sure. Anything might be happening. He might strike her from above—with one of those heavy boots perhaps. Nothing seemed to be happening, but the suspense was intolerable. She realized now that she hadn't the power to endure a night of it. Anything would be better than this—disgrace, imprisonment, even death. She would crawl out, wake the man, and try and explain as best she could.

She would switch on the light, cough, and say: '*Monsieur!*'

Then he would start up and stare at her.

Then she would say—what should she say?

'*Pardon, monsieur, mais je*——' What on earth was the French for 'I have made a mistake'?

'*J'ai tort. C'est la chambre*—er—incorrect. *Voulez-vous*—er——'

What was the French for 'door-knob', 'let me go'?

It didn't matter. She would turn on the light, cough and trust to luck. If he got out of bed, and came towards her, she would scream the hotel down. . . .

The resolution formed, she crawled deliberately out at the foot of the bed. She scrambled hastily towards the door—a perilous journey. In a few seconds the room was flooded with light. She turned towards the bed, coughed, and cried out boldly:

'*Monsieur!*'

Then, for the third time that night, little Miss Bracegirdle's heart all but stopped. In this case the climax of the horror took longer to develop, but when it was reached, it clouded the other two experiences into insignificance.

The man on the bed was dead!

She had never beheld death before, but one does not mistake death.

She stared at him bewildered, and repeated almost in a whisper:
'*Monsieur! . . . Monsieur!*'

Then she tiptoed towards the bed. The hair and moustache looked extraordinarily black in that grey, wax-like setting. The mouth was slightly open, and the face, which in life might have been vicious and sensual, looked incredibly peaceful and far away.

It was as though she were regarding the features of a man across some vast passage of time, a being who had always been completely remote from mundane preoccupations.

When the full truth came home to her, little Miss Bracegirdle buried her face in her hands and murmured:

'Poor fellow ... poor fellow!'

For the moment her own position seemed an affair of small consequence. She was in the presence of something greater and more all-pervading. Almost instinctively she knelt by the bed and prayed.

For a few moments she seemed to be possessed by an extraordinary calmness and detachment. The burden of her hotel predicament was a gossamer trouble—a silly, trivial, almost comic episode, something that could be explained away.

But this man—he had lived his life, whatever it was like, now he was in the presence of his Maker. What kind of man had he been?

Her meditations were broken by an abrupt sound. It was that of a pair of heavy boots being thrown down by the door outside. She started, thinking at first it was someone knocking or trying to get in. She heard the 'boots', however, stumping away down the corridor, and the realization stabbed her with the truth of her own position. She mustn't stop there. The necessity to get out was even more urgent.

To be found in a strange man's bedroom in the night is bad enough, but to be found in a dead man's bedroom was even worse. They could accuse her of murder, perhaps. Yes, that would be it— how could she possibly explain to these foreigners? Good God! they would hang her. No, guillotine her, that's what they do in France. They would chop her head off with a great steel knife. Merciful heavens! She envisaged herself standing blindfold, by a priest and an executioner in a red cap, like that man in the Dickens story— what was his name? ... Sydney Carton, that was it, and before he went on the scaffold he said:

'It is a far, far better thing that I do than I have ever done.'

But no, she couldn't say that. It would be a far, far worse thing that she did. What about the dear dean? Her sister-in-law arriving alone from Paraguay tomorrow? All her dear people and friends in Easingstoke? Her darling Tony, the large grey tabby cat? It was her duty not to have her head chopped off if it could possibly be avoided. She could do no good in the room. She could not recall the dead to life. Her only mission was to escape. Any minute people might arrive. The chambermaid, the boots, the manager, the gendarmes.... Visions of gendarmes arriving armed with swords and note-books vitalized her almost exhausted energies. She was a desperate woman. Fortunately now she had not to worry about the light. She sprang once more at the door and tried to force it open with her fingers. The result hurt her and gave her pause. If she was to escape she must *think*, and think intensely. She mustn't do anything rash and silly, she must just think and plan calmly.

She examined the lock carefully. There was no keyhole, but there was a slip-bolt, so that the hotel guest could lock the door on the inside, but it couldn't be locked on the outside. Oh, why didn't this poor dear dead man lock his door last night? Then this trouble could not have happened. She could see the end of the steel pin. It was about half an inch down the hole. If anyone was passing they must surely notice the handle sticking out too far the other side! She drew a hairpin out of her hair and tried to coax the pin back, but she only succeeded in pushing it a little farther in. She felt the colour leaving her face, and a strange feeling of faintness come over her.

She was fighting for her life, she mustn't give way. She darted round the room like an animal in a trap, her mind alert for the slightest crevice of escape. The window had no balcony and there was a drop of five storeys to the street below. Dawn was breaking. Soon the activities of the hotel and the city would begin. The thing must be accomplished before then.

She went back once more and stared at the lock. She stared at the dead man's property, his razors, and brushes, and writing materials, pens and pencils and rubber and sealing-wax.... Sealing-wax!

Necessity is truly the mother of invention. It is in any case quite certain that Millicent Bracegirdle, who had never invented a thing in her life, would never have evolved the ingenious little device she did, had she not believed that her position was utterly desperate. For in the end this is what she did. She got together a box of matches, a candle, a bar of sealing-wax, and a hairpin. She made a little pool of hot sealing-wax, into which she dipped the end of the hairpin. Collecting a small blob on the end of it she thrust it into the hole, and let it adhere to the end of the steel pin. At the seventh attempt she got the thing to move. It took her just an hour and ten minutes to get that steel pin back into the room, and when at length it came far enough through for her to grip it with her finger-nails, she burst into tears through the sheer physical tension of the strain. Very, very carefully she pulled it through, and holding it firmly with her left hand she fixed the knob with her right, then slowly turned it. The door opened!

The temptation to dash out into the corridor and scream with relief was almost irresistible, but she forbore. She listened; she peeped out. No one was about. With beating heart, she went out, closing the door inaudibly. She crept like a little mouse to the room next door, stole in and flung herself on her bed. Immediately she did so it flashed through her mind that *she had left her sponge-bag and towel in the dead man's room*!

In looking back upon her experience she always considered that that second expedition was the worst of all. She might have left the sponge-bag and towel there, only that the towel—she never used hotel towels—had neatly inscribed in the corner 'M.B.'

With furtive caution she managed to retrace her steps. She re-entered the dead man's room, reclaimed her property, and returned to her own. When this mission was accomplished she was indeed wellnigh spent. She lay on her bed and groaned feebly. At last she fell into a fevered sleep. . . .

It was eleven o'clock when she awoke and no one had been to disturb her. The sun was shining, and the experiences of the night appeared a dubious nightmare. Surely she had dreamt it all?

With dread still burning in her heart she rang the bell. After a short interval of time the chambermaid appeared. The girl's eyes were bright with some uncontrollable excitement. No, she had not been dreaming. This girl had heard something.

'Will you bring me some tea, please?'

'Certainly, madame.'

The maid drew back the curtains and fussed about the room. She was under a pledge of secrecy, but she could contain herself no longer. Suddenly she approached the bed and whispered excitedly:

'Oh, madame, I have promised not to tell . . . but a terrible thing has happened. A man, a dead man, has been found in room 117— a guest. Please not to say I tell you. But they have all been there, the gendarmes, the doctors, the inspectors. Oh, it is terrible . . . terrible.'

The little lady in the bed said nothing. There was indeed nothing to say. But Marie Louise Lancret was too full of emotional excitement to spare her.

'But the terrible thing is—— Do you know who he was, madame? They say it is Boldhu, the man wanted for the murder of Jeanne Carreton in the barn at Vincennes. They say he strangled her, and then cut her up in pieces and hid her in two barrels which he threw into the river. . . . Oh, but he was a bad man, madame, a terrible bad man . . . and he died in the room next door . . . suicide, they think; or was it an attack of the heart? . . . Remorse, some shock perhaps. . . . Did you say a *café complet*, madame?'

'No, thank you, my dear . . . just a cup of tea . . . strong tea. . . .'

'*Parfaitement*, madame.'

The girl retired, and a little later a waiter entered the room with a tray of tea. She could never get over her surprise at this. It seemed so—well, indecorous for a man—although only a waiter—to enter a lady's bedroom. There was no doubt a great deal in what the dear dean said. They were certainly very peculiar, these French people—they had most peculiar notions. It was not the way they behaved at Easingstoke. She got farther under the sheets, but the waiter appeared quite indifferent to the situation. He put the tray down and retired.

When he had gone she sat up and sipped her tea, which gradually warmed her. She was glad the sun was shining. She would have to get up soon. They said that her sister-in-law's boat was due to berth at one o'clock. That would give her time to dress comfortably, write to her brother, and then go down to the docks. Poor man! So he had been a murderer, a man who cut up the bodies of his victims . . . and she had spent the night in his bedroom! They were certainly a most—how could she describe it?—people. Nevertheless she felt a little glad that at the end she had been there to kneel and pray by his bedside. Probably nobody else had ever done that. It was very difficult to judge people. . . . Something at some time might have gone wrong. He might not have murdered the woman after all. People were often wrongly convicted. She herself. . . . If the police had found her in that room at three o'clock that morning. . . . It is that which takes place in the heart which counts. One learns and learns. Had she not learnt that one can pray just as effectively lying under a bed as kneeling beside it? . . . Poor man!

She washed and dressed herself and walked calmly down to the writing-room. There was no evidence of excitement among the other hotel guests. Probably none of them knew about the tragedy except herself. She went to a writing-table, and after profound meditation wrote as follows:

'My dear Brother,

'I arrived late last night after a very pleasant journey. Everyone was very kind and attentive, the manager was sitting up for me. I nearly lost my spectacle case in the restaurant car! But a kind old gentleman found it and returned it to me. There was a most amusing American child on the train. I will tell you about her on my return. The people are very pleasant, but the food is peculiar, nothing *plain and wholesome.* I am going down to meet Annie at one o'clock. How have you been keeping, my dear? I hope you have not had any further return of the bronchial attacks.

'Please tell Lizzie that I remembered in the train on the way here that that large stone jar of marmalade that Mrs Hunt made is behind those empty tins on the top shelf of the cupboard next to the coach-house. I wonder whether Mrs Butler was able to come to evensong after all? This is a nice hotel, but I think Annie and I will stay at the "Grand" tonight, as the bedrooms here are rather noisy. Well, my dear, nothing more till I return. Do take care of yourself.—Your loving sister,

'Millicent.'

Yes, she couldn't tell Peter about it; neither in the letter nor when she went back to him. It was her duty not to tell him. It would only distress him; she felt convinced of it. In this curious foreign atmosphere the thing appeared possible, but in Easingstoke the mere recounting of the fantastic situations would be positively . . . indelicate.

There was no escaping that broad general fact—she had spent a night in a strange man's bedroom. Whether he was a gentleman or a criminal, even whether he was dead or alive, did not seem to mitigate the jar upon her sensibilities, or rather it would not mitigate the jar upon the peculiarly sensitive relationship between her brother and herself. To say that she had been to the bathroom, the knob of the door-handle came off in her hand, she was too frightened to awaken the sleeper or scream, she got under the bed— well, it was all perfectly true. Peter would believe her, but—one simply could not conceive such a situation in Easingstoke deanery. It would create a curious little barrier between them, as though she had been dipped in some mysterious solution which alienated her. It was her duty not to tell.

She put on her hat, and went out to post the letter. She distrusted an hotel letter-box. One never knew who handled these letters. It was not a proper official way of treating them. She walked to the head post office in Bordeaux.

The sun was shining. It was very pleasant walking about amongst these queer excitable people, so foreign and different-looking—and the cafés already crowded with chattering men and women, and the flower stalls, and the strange odour of—what was it? Salt? Brine? Charcoal?... A military band was playing in the square ... very gay and moving. It was all life, and movement, and bustle ... thrilling rather.

'I spent a night in a strange man's bedroom.'

Little Miss Bracegirdle hunched her shoulders, murmured to herself, and walked faster. She reached the post office and found the large metal plate with the slot for letters and 'RF' stamped above it. Something official at last! Her face was a little flushed—was it the warmth of the day or the contact of movement and life?—as she put her letter into the slot. After posting it she put her hand into the slot and flicked it round to see that there were no foreign contraptions to impede its safe delivery. No, the letter had dropped safely in. She sighed contentedly and walked off in the direction of the docks to meet her sister-in-law from Paraguay.

The Story-Teller

It was a hot afternoon, and the railway carriage was correspondingly sultry, and the next stop was at Templecombe, nearly an hour ahead. The occupants of the carriage were a small girl, and a smaller girl, and a small boy. An aunt belonging to the children occupied one corner seat, and the further corner seat on the opposite side was occupied by a bachelor who was a stranger to their party, but the small girls and the small boy emphatically occupied the compartment. Both the aunt and the children were conversational in a limited, persistent way, reminding one of the attentions of a housefly that refused to be discouraged. Most of the aunt's remarks seemed to begin with 'Don't', and nearly all of the children's remarks began with 'Why?' The bachelor said nothing out loud.

'Don't, Cyril, don't,' exclaimed the aunt, as the small boy began smacking the cushions of the seat, producing a cloud of dust at each blow.

'Come and look out of the window,' she added.

The child moved reluctantly to the window. 'Why are those sheep being driven out of that field?' he asked.

'I expect they are being driven to another field where there is more grass,' said the aunt weakly.

'But there is lots of grass in that field,' protested the boy; 'there's nothing else but grass there. Aunt, there's lots of grass in that field.'

'Perhaps the grass in the other field is better,' suggested the aunt fatuously.

'Why is it better?' came the swift, inevitable question.

'Oh, look at those cows!' exclaimed the aunt. Nearly every field along the line had contained cows or bullocks, but she spoke as though she were drawing attention to a rarity.

'Why is the grass in the other field better?' persisted Cyril.

The frown on the bachelor's face was deepening to a scowl. He was a hard, unsympathetic man, the aunt decided in her mind. She was utterly unable to come to any satisfactory decision about the grass in the other field.

The smaller girl created a diversion by beginning to recite 'On the Road to Mandalay'. She only knew the first line, but she put her limited knowledge to the fullest possible use. She repeated the line over and over again in a dreamy but resolute and very audible voice; it seemed to the bachelor as though someone had had a bet with her that she could not repeat the line aloud 2000 times without stopping. Whoever it was who made the wager was likely to lose his bet.

'Come over here and listen to a story,' said the aunt, when the bachelor had looked twice at her and once at the communication cord.

The children moved listlessly towards the aunt's end of the carriage. Evidently her reputation as a story-teller did not rank high in their estimation.

In a low, confidential voice, interrupted at frequent intervals by loud, petulant questions from her listeners, she began an unenterprising and deplorably uninteresting story about a little girl who was good, and made friends with everyone on account of her goodness, and was finally saved from a mad bull by a number of rescuers who admired her moral character.

'Wouldn't they have saved her if she hadn't been good?' demanded the bigger of the small girls. It was exactly the question that the bachelor had wanted to ask.

'Well, yes,' admitted the aunt lamely, 'but I don't think they would have run quite so fast to her help if they had not liked her so much.'

'It's the stupidest story I've every heard,' said the bigger of the small girls, with immense conviction.

'I didn't listen after the first bit, it was so stupid,' said Cyril.

The smaller girl made no actual comment on the story, but she had long ago recommenced a murmured repetition of her favourite line.

'You don't seem to be a success as a story-teller,' said the bachelor suddenly from his corner.

The aunt bristled in instant defence at this unexpected attack.

'It's a very difficult thing to tell stories that children can both understand and appreciate,' she said stiffly.

'I don't agree with you,' said the bachelor.

'Perhaps *you* would like to tell them a story,' was the aunt's retort.

'Tell us a story,' demanded the bigger of the small girls.

'Once upon a time,' began the bachelor, 'there was a little girl called Bertha, who was extraordinarily good.'

The children's momentarily-aroused interest began at once to flicker; all stories seemed dreadfully alike, no matter who told them.

'She did all that she was told, she was always truthful, she kept her clothes clean, ate milk puddings as though they were jam tarts, learned her lessons perfectly, and was polite in her manners.'

'Was she pretty?' asked the bigger of the small girls.

'Not as pretty as any of you,' said the bachelor, 'but she was horribly good.'

There was a wave of reaction in favour of the story; the word horrible in connection with goodness was a novelty that commended itself. It seemed to introduce a ring of truth that was absent from the aunt's tales of infant life.

'She was so good,' continued the bachelor, 'that she won several medals for goodness, which she always wore, pinned on to her dress. There was a medal for obedience, another medal for punctuality, and a third for good behaviour. They were large metal medals and they clicked against one another as she walked. No other child in the town where she lived had as many as three medals, so everybody knew that she must be an extra-good child.'

'Horribly good,' quoted Cyril.

'Everybody talked about her goodness, and the Prince of the country got to hear about it, and he said that as she was so very good she might be allowed once a week to walk in his park, which was just outside the town. It was a beautiful park, and no children were ever allowed in it, so it was a great honour for Bertha to be allowed to go there.'

'Were there any sheep in the park?' demanded Cyril.

'No,' said the bachelor, 'there were no sheep.'

'Why weren't there any sheep?' came the inevitable question arising out of that answer.

The aunt permitted herself a smile, which might almost have been described as a grin.

'There were no sheep in the park,' said the bachelor, 'because the Prince's mother had once had a dream that her son would either be killed by a sheep or else by a clock falling on him. For that reason the Prince never kept a sheep in his park or a clock in his palace.'

The aunt suppressed a gasp of admiration.

'Was the Prince killed by a sheep or by a clock?' asked Cyril.

'He is still alive, so we can't tell whether the dream will come true,' said the bachelor unconcernedly; 'anyway, there were no sheep in the park, but there were lots of little pigs running all over the place.'

'What colour were they?'

'Black with white faces, white with black spots, black all over, grey with white patches, and some were white all over.'

The story-teller paused to let a full idea of the park's treasures sink into the children's imaginations; then he resumed:

'Bertha was rather sorry to find that there were no flowers in the park. She had promised her aunts, with tears in her eyes, that she would not pick any of the kind Prince's flowers, and she had meant to keep her promise, so of course it made her feel silly to find that there were no flowers to pick.'

'Why weren't there any flowers?'

'Because the pigs had eaten them all,' said the bachelor promptly. 'The gardeners had told the Prince that you couldn't have pigs and flowers, so he decided to have pigs and no flowers.'

There was a murmur of approval at the excellence of the Prince's decision; so many people would have decided the other way.

'There were lots of other delightful things in the park. There were ponds with gold and blue and green fish in them, and trees with beautiful parrots that said clever things at a moment's notice, and humming birds that hummed all the popular tunes of the day. Bertha walked up and down and enjoyed herself immensely, and thought to herself: "If I were not so extraordinarily good I should not have been allowed to come into this beautiful park and enjoy all that there is to be seen in it," and her three medals clinked against one another as she walked and helped to remind her how very good she really was. Just then an enormous wolf came prowling into the park to see if it could catch a fat little pig for its supper.'

'What colour was it?' asked the children, amid an immediate quickening of interest.

'Mud-colour all over, with a black tongue and pale grey eyes that gleamed with unspeakable ferocity. The first thing that it saw in the park was Bertha; her pinafore was so spotlessly white and clean that it could be seen from a great distance. Bertha saw the wolf and saw that it was stealing towards her, and she began to wish that she had never been allowed to come into the park. She ran as hard as she could, and the wolf came after her with huge leaps and bounds. She managed to reach a shrubbery of myrtle bushes and she hid herself in one of the thickest of the bushes. The wolf came sniffing among the branches, its black tongue lolling out of its mouth and its pale grey eyes glaring with rage. Bertha was terribly frightened, and thought to herself: "If I had not been so extraordinarily good I should have been safe in the town at this moment." However, the scent of the myrtle was so strong that the wolf could not sniff out where Bertha was hiding, and the bushes were so thick that he might have hunted about in them for a long time without catching sight of her, so he thought he might as well go off and catch a little pig instead. Bertha was trembling very much at having the wolf prowling and sniffing so near her, and as she trembled the medal for obedience clinked against the medals for good conduct and punctuality. The wolf was just moving away when he heard the sound of the medals clinking and stopped to listen; they clinked again in a bush quite near him. He dashed into the bush, his pale grey eyes gleaming with ferocity and triumph, and dragged Bertha out and devoured her to the last morsel. All that was left of her were her shoes, bits of clothing, and the three medals for goodness.'

'Were any of the little pigs killed?'

'No, they all escaped.'

'The story began badly,' said the smaller of the small girls, 'but it had a beautiful ending.'

'It is the most beautiful story that I ever heard,' said the bigger of the small girls, with immense decision.

'It is the *only* beautiful story I have ever heard,' said Cyril.

A dissentient opinion came from the aunt.

'A most improper story to tell to young children! You have undermined the effect of years of careful teaching.'

'At any rate,' said the bachelor, collecting his belongings preparatory to leaving the carriage, 'I kept them quiet for ten minutes, which was more than you were able to do.'

'Unhappy woman!' he observed to himself as he walked down the platform of Templecombe station; 'for the next six months or so those children will assail her in public with demands for an improper story!'

W. W. Jacobs

An Elaborate Elopement

I have always had a slight suspicion that the following narrative is not quite true. It was related to me by an old seaman who, among other incidents of a somewhat adventurous career, claimed to have received Napoleon's sword at the battle of Trafalgar, and a wound in the back at Waterloo. I prefer to tell it in my own way, his being so garnished with nautical terms and expletives as to be half unintelligible and somewhat horrifying. Our talk had been of love and courtship, and after making me a present of several tips, invented by himself, and considered invaluable by his friends, he related this story of the courtship of a chum of his as illustrating the great lengths to which young bloods were prepared to go in his days to attain their ends.

It was a fine clear day in June when Hezekiah Lewis, captain and part owner of the schooner *Thames*, bound from London to Aberdeen, anchored off the little out-of-the-way town of Orford in Suffolk. Among other antiquities, the town possessed Hezekiah's widowed mother, and when there was no very great hurry—the world went slower in those days—the dutiful son used to go ashore in the ship's boat, and after a filial tap at his mother's window, which often startled the old woman considerably, pass on his way to see a young lady to whom he had already proposed five times without effect.

The mate and crew of the schooner, seven all told, drew up in a little knot as the skipper, in his shore-going clothes, appeared on deck, and regarded him with an air of grinning, mysterious interest.

'Now you all know what you have got to do?' queried the skipper.

'Ay, ay,' replied the crew, grinning still more deeply.

Hezekiah regarded them closely, and then ordering the boat to be lowered, scrambled over the side, and was pulled swiftly towards the shore.

A sharp scream, and a breathless 'Lawk-a-mussy me!' as he tapped at his mother's window, assured him that the old lady was alive and well, and he continued on his way until he brought up at a small but pretty house in the next road.

'Morning, Mr Rumbolt,' said he heartily to a stout, red-faced man, who sat smoking in the doorway.

'Morning, cap'n, morning,' said the red-faced man.

'Is the rheumatism any better?' inquired Hezekiah anxiously, as he grasped the other's huge hand.

'So, so,' said the other. 'But it ain't the rheumatism so much what troubles me,' he resumed, lowering his voice, and looking round cautiously. 'It's Kate.'

'What?' said the skipper.

'You've heard of a man being henpecked?' continued Mr Rumbolt, in tones of husky confidence.

The captain nodded.

'I'm *chick-pecked*,' murmured the other.

'What?' inquired the astonished mariner again.

'Chick-pecked,' repeated Mr Rumbolt firmly. 'CHIK-PEKED. D'ye understand me?'

The captain said that he did, and stood silent awhile, with the air of a man who wants to say something, but is half afraid to. At last, with a desperate appearance of resolution, he bent down to the old man's ear.

'That's the deaf 'un,' said Mr Rumbolt promptly.

Hezekiah changed ears, speaking at first slowly and awkwardly, but becoming more fluent as he warmed with his subject; while the expression of his listener's face gradually changed from incredulous bewilderment to one of uncontrollable mirth. He became so uproarious that he was fain to push the captain away from him, and lean back in his chair and choke and laugh until he nearly lost his breath, at which crisis a remarkably pretty girl appeared from the back of the house, and patted him with hearty good will.

'That'll do, my dear,' said the choking Mr Rumbolt. 'Here's Captain Lewis.'

'I can see him,' said his daughter calmly. 'What's he standing on one leg for?'

The skipper, who really was standing in a somewhat constrained attitude, coloured violently, and planted both feet firmly on the ground.

'Being as I was passing close in, Miss Rumbolt,' said he, 'and coming ashore to see mother——'

To the captain's discomfort, manifestations of a further attack on the part of Mr Rumbolt appeared, but were promptly quelled by the daughter.

'Mother?' she repeated encouragingly.

'I thought I'd come on and ask you just to pay a sort o' flying visit to the *Thames*.'

'Thank you, I'm comfortable enough where I am,' said the girl.

'I've got a couple of monkeys and a bear aboard, which I'm taking to a menagerie in Aberdeen,' continued the captain, 'and the thought struck me you might possibly like to see 'em.'

'Well, I don't know,' said the damsel in a flutter. 'Is it a big bear?'

'Have you ever seen an elephant?' inquired Hezekiah cautiously.

'Only in pictures,' replied the girl.

'Well, it's as big as that, nearly,' said he.

The temptation was irresistible, and Miss Rumbolt, telling her father that she should not be long, disappeared into the house in search of her hat and jacket, and ten minutes later the brawny rowers were gazing their fill into her deep blue eyes as she sat in the stern of the boat, and told Lewis to behave himself.

It was but a short pull out to the schooner, and Miss Rumbolt was soon on the deck, lavishing endearments on the monkey, and energetically prodding the bear with a handspike to make him growl. The noise of the offended animal as he strove to get through the bars of his cage was terrific, and the girl was in the full enjoyment of it, when she became aware of a louder noise still, and, turning round, saw the seamen at the windlass.

'Why, what are they doing?' she demanded. 'Getting up anchor?'

'Ahoy, there!' shouted Hezekiah sternly. 'What are you doing with that windlass?'

As he spoke, the anchor peeped over the edge of the bows, and one of the seamen running past them took the helm.

'Now then,' shouted the fellow, 'stand by. Look lively there with them sails.'

Obeying a light touch of the helm, the schooner's bow-sprit slowly swung round from the land, and the crew, hauling lustily on the ropes, began to hoist the sails.

'What the devil are you up to?' thundered the skipper. 'Have you all gone mad? What does it all mean?'

'It means,' said one of the seamen, whose fat, amiable face was marred by a fearful scowl, 'that we've got a new skipper.'

'Good heavens, a mutiny!' exclaimed the skipper, starting melo-dramatically against the cage, and starting hastily away again. 'Where's the mate?'

'He's with us,' said another seaman, brandishing his sheath knife, and scowling fearfully. 'He's our new captain.'

In confirmation of this the mate now appeared from below with an axe in his hand, and, approaching his captain, roughly ordered him below.

'I'll defend this lady with my life,' cried Hezekiah, taking the handspike from Kate, and raising it above his head.

'Nobody'll hurt a hair of her beautiful head,' said the mate, with a tender smile.

'Then I yield,' said the skipper, drawing himself up, and deliver-ing the handspike with the air of a defeated admiral tendering his sword.

'Good,' said the mate briefly, as one of the men took it.

'What!' demanded Miss Rumbolt excitedly. 'Aren't you going to fight them? Here, give me the handspike.'

Before the mate could interfere, the sailor, with thoughtless obedience, handed it over, and Miss Rumbolt at once tried to knock him over the head. Being thwarted in this design by the man taking flight, she lost her temper entirely, and bore down like a hurricane on the remaining members of the crew who were just approaching.

They scattered at once, and ran up the rigging like cats, and for a few moments the girl held the deck; then the mate crept up behind her, and with the air of a man whose job exactly suited him, clasped her tightly round the waist, while one of the seamen disarmed her.

'You must both go below till we've settled what to do with you,' said the mate, reluctantly releasing her.

With a wistful glance at the handspike the girl walked to the cabin, followed slowly by the skipper.

'This is a bad business,' said the latter, shaking his head solemnly, as the indignant Miss Rumbolt seated herself.

'Don't talk to me, you coward!' said the girl energetically.

The skipper started.

'*I* made three of 'em run,' said Miss Rumbolt, 'and you did nothing. You just stood still, and let them take the ship. I'm ashamed of you.'

The skipper's defence was interrupted by a hoarse voice shouting to them to come on deck, where they found the mutinous crew gathered aft round the mate. The girl cast a look at the shore, which was now dim and indistinct, and turned somewhat pale as the serious nature of her position forced itself upon her.

'Lewis,' said the mate.

'Well,' growled the skipper.

'This ship's going in the lace and brandy trade, and if so be as you're sensible you can go with it as mate, d'ye hear?'

'An' s'pose I do; what about the lady?' inquired the captain.

'You and the lady'll have to get spliced,' said the mate sternly. 'Then there'll be no tales told. A Scotch marriage is as good as any, and we'll just lay off and put you ashore, and you can get tied up as right as ninepence.'

'Marry a coward like that?' demanded Miss Rumbolt, with spirit; 'not if I know it. Why, I'd sooner marry that old man at the helm.'

'Old Bill's got three wives a'ready to my sartin knowledge,' spoke up one of the sailors. 'The lady's got to marry Cap'n Lewis, so don't let's have no fuss about it.'

'I won't,' said the lady, stamping violently.

The mutineers appeared to be in a dilemma, and, following the example of the mate, scratched their heads thoughtfully.

'We thought you liked him,' said the mate, at last, feebly.

'You had no business to think,' said Miss Rumbolt. 'You are bad men, and you'll all be hung, every one of you; I shall come and see it.'

'The cap'n's welcome to her for me,' murmured the helmsman in a husky whisper to the man next to him. 'The vixen!'

'Very good,' said the mate. 'If you won't, you won't. This end of the ship'll belong to you after eight o'clock of a night. Lewis, you must go for'ard with the men.'

'And what are you going to do with me after?' inquired the fair prisoner.

The seven men shrugged their shoulders helplessly, and Hezekiah, looking depressed, lit his pipe, and went and leaned over the side.

The day passed quietly. The orders were given by the mate, and Hezekiah lounged moodily about, a prisoner at large. At eight o'clock Miss Rumbolt was given the key of the stateroom, and the men who were not in the watch went below.

The morning broke fine and clear with a light breeze, which, towards midday, dropped entirely, and the schooner lay rocking lazily on a sea of glassy smoothness. The sun beat fiercely down, bringing the fresh paint on the taffrail up in blisters, and sorely trying the tempers of the men who were doing odd jobs on deck.

The cabin, where the two victims of a mutinous crew had retired for coolness, got more and more stuffy, until at length even the scorching deck seemed preferable, and the girl, with a faint hope of finding a shady corner, went languidly up the companion-ladder.

For some time the skipper sat alone, pondering gloomily over the state of affairs as he smoked his short pipe. He was aroused at length from his apathy by the sound of the companion being noisily closed, while loud frightened cries and hurrying footsteps on deck announced that something extraordinary was happening. As he rose to his feet he was confronted by Kate Rumbolt, who, panting and excited, waved a big key before him.

'I've done it,' she cried, her eyes sparkling.

'Done what?' shouted the mystified skipper.

'Let the bear loose,' said the girl. 'Ha, ha! you should have seen them run. You should have seen the fat sailor!'

'Let the—phew—let the—— Good Heavens! here's a pretty kettle of fish!' he choked.

'Listen to them shouting,' cried the exultant Kate, clapping her hands. 'Just listen.'

'Those shouts are from aloft,' said Hezekiah sternly, 'where you and I ought to be.'

'I've closed the companion,' said the girl reassuringly.

'Closed the companion!' repeated Hezekiah, as he drew his knife. 'He can smash it like cardboard, if the fit takes him. Go in here.'

He opened the door of his stateroom.

'Shan't!' said Miss Rumbolt politely.

'Go in at once!' cried the skipper. 'Quick with you.'

'Sha—' began Miss Rumbolt again. Then she caught his eye, and went in like a lamb. 'You come too,' she said prettily.

'I've got to look after my ship and my men,' said the skipper. 'I suppose you thought the ship would steer itself, didn't you?'

'Mutineers deserve to be eaten,' whimpered Miss Rumbolt piously, somewhat taken aback by the skipper's demeanour.

Hezekiah looked at her.

'They're not mutineers, Kate,' he said quietly. 'It was just a piece of mad folly of mine. They're as honest a set of old sea dogs as ever breathed, and I only hope they are all safe up aloft. I'm going to lock you in; but don't be frightened, it shan't hurt you.'

He slammed the door on her protests, and locked it, and, slipping the key of the cage in his pocket, took a firm grip of his knife, and, running up the steps, gained the deck. Then his breath came more freely, for the mate, who was standing a little way up the fore rigging, after tempting the bear with his foot, had succeeded in dropping a noose over its head. The brute made a furious attempt to extricate itself, but the men hurried down with other lines, and in a short space of time the bear presented much the same appearance as the lion in *Æsop's Fables*, and was dragged and pushed, a heated and indignant mass of fur, back to its cage.

Having locked up one prisoner the skipper went below and released the other, who passed quickly from a somewhat hysterical condition to one of such haughty disdain that the captain was thoroughly cowed, and stood humbly aside to let her pass.

The fat seaman was standing in front of the cage as she reached it, and regarding the bear with much satisfaction until Kate sidled up to him, and begged him, as a personal favour, to go in the cage and undo it.

'Undo it! Why, he'd kill me!' gasped the fat seaman, aghast at such simplicity.

'I don't think he would,' said his tormentor, with a bewitching smile; 'and I'll wear a lock of your hair all my life if you do. But you'd better give it to me before you go in.'

'I ain't going in,' said the fat sailor shortly.

'Not for me?' queried Kate archly.

'Not for fifty like you,' replied the old man firmly. 'He nearly had me when he was loose. I can't think how he got out.'

'Why, I let him out,' said Miss Rumbolt airily. 'Just for a little run. How would you like to be shut up all day?'

The sailor was just going to tell her with more fluency than politeness when he was interrupted.

'That'll do,' said the skipper, who had come behind them. 'Go for'ard, you. There's been enough of this fooling; the lady thought you had taken the ship. Thompson, I'll take the helm; there's a little wind coming. Stand by there.'

He walked aft and relieved the steersman, awkwardly conscious that the men were becoming more and more interested in the situation, and also that Kate could hear some of their remarks. As he pondered over the subject, and tried to think of a way out of it, the cause of all the trouble came and stood by him.

'Did my father know of this?' she inquired.

'I don't know that he did exactly,' said the skipper uneasily. 'I just told him not to expect you back that night.'

'And what did he say?' said she.

'Said he wouldn't sit up,' said the skipper, grinning, despite himself.

Kate drew a breath the length of which boded no good to her parent, and looked over the side.

'I was afraid of that traveller chap from Ipswich,' said Hezekiah, after a pause. 'Your father told me he was hanging round you again, so I thought I—well, I was a blamed fool anyway.'

'See how ridiculous you have made me look before all these men,' said the girl angrily.

'They've been with me for years,' said Hezekiah apologetically, 'and the mate said it was a magnificent idea. He quite raved about it, he did. I wouldn't have done it with some crews, but we've had some dirty times together, and they've stood by me well. But of course that's nothing to do with you. It's been an adventure I'm very sorry for, very.'

'A pretty safe adventure for *you*,' said the girl scornfully. '*You* didn't risk much. Look here, I like brave men. If you go in the cage and undo that bear, I'll marry you. That's what *I* call an adventure.'

'Smith,' called the skipper quietly, 'come and take the helm a bit.'

The seaman obeyed, and Lewis, accompanied by the girl, walked forward.

At the bear's cage he stopped, and, fumbling in his pocket for the key, steadily regarded the brute as it lay gnashing its teeth, and trying in vain to bite the ropes which bound it.

'You're afraid,' said the girl tauntingly; 'you're quite white.'

The captain made no reply, but eyed her so steadily that her gaze fell. He drew the key from his pocket and inserted it in the huge lock, and was just turning it, when a soft arm was drawn through his, and a soft voice murmured sweetly in his ear, 'Never mind about the old bear.'

And he did not mind.

Under the Deck-Awnings

'Can any man—a gentleman, I mean—call a woman a pig?' The little man flung this challenge forth to the whole group, then leaned back in his deckchair, sipping lemonade with an air commingled of certitude and watchful belligerence. Nobody made answer. They were used to the little man and his sudden passions and high elevations.

'I repeat, it was in my presence that he said a certain lady, whom none of you knows, was a pig. He did not say swine. He grossly said that she was a pig. And I hold that no man who is a man could possibly make such a remark about any woman.'

Doctor Dawson puffed stolidly at his black pipe. Matthews, with knees hunched up and clasped by his arms, was absorbed in the flight of a guny. Sweet, finishing his Scotch and soda, was questing about with his eyes for a deck-steward.

'I ask you, Mr Treloar, can any man call a woman a pig?'

Treloar, who happened to be sitting next to him, was startled by the abruptness of the attack, and wondered what grounds he had ever given the little man to believe that he could call a woman a pig.

'I should say,' he began his hesitant answer, 'that it—er—depends on the—er—the lady.'

The little man was aghast.

'You mean—' he quavered.

'That I have seen female humans who were as bad as pigs—and worse.'

There was a long, painful silence. The little man seemed withered by the coarse brutality of the reply. In his face was unutterable hurt and woe.

'You have told of a man who made a not nice remark, and you have classified him,' Treloar said in cold, even tones. 'I shall now tell you about a woman—I beg your pardon—a lady—and when I have finished I shall ask you to classify her. Miss Caruthers I shall call her, principally for the reason that it is not her name. It was on a P & O boat, and it occurred several years ago.

'Miss Caruthers was charming. No; that is not the word. She was amazing. She was a young woman and a lady. Her father was a certain high official whose name, if I mentioned it, would be immediately recognized by all of you. She was with her mother and two maids at the time, going out to join the old gentleman wherever you like to wish in the East.

'She—and pardon me for repeating—was amazing. It is the one adequate word. Even the most minor adjectives applicable to her are bound to be sheer superlatives. There was nothing she could not do better than any woman and than most men. Sing, play— bah!—as some rhetorician once said of old Nap, competition fled from her. Swim! She could have made a fortune and a name as a public performer. She was one of those rare women who can strip off all the frills of dress and in a simple swimming suit be more satisfyingly beautiful. Dress! She was an artist. Her taste was unerring.

'But her swimming. Physically, she was the perfect woman— you know what I mean; not in the gross, muscular way of acrobats, but in all the delicacy of line and fragility of frame and texture; and combined with this, strength. How she could do it was the marvel. You know the wonder of a woman's arm—the forearm, I mean; the sweet fading away from rounded biceps and hint of muscle, down through small elbow and firm, soft swell to the wrist, small—unthinkably small and round and strong? This was hers. And yet, to see her swimming the sharp, quick English overhand stroke, and getting somewhere with it too, was—well, I understand anatomy and athletics and such things, and yet it was a mystery to me how she could do it.

'She could stay under water for two minutes. I have timed her. No man on board, except Dennitson, could capture as many coins as she with a single dive. On the forward main deck was a big canvas tank with six feet of sea-water. We used to toss small coins into it. I have seen her dive from the bridge deck—no mean feat in itself—into that six feet of water and fetch up no less than forty-seven coins, scattered at random over the whole bottom of the tank. Dennitson, a quiet young Englishman, never exceeded her in this, though he made it a point always to tie her score.

'She was a seawoman, true. But she was a landwoman, a horse-woman—a—she was the universal woman. To see her, all softness of flowing dress, surrounded by half a dozen eager men, languidly careless of them, or flashing brightness and wit on them and at them and through them, one would fancy she was good for nothing else in the world. At such moments I have compelled myself to remember her score of forty-seven coins from the bottom of the swimming tank. But that was she—the everlasting wonder of a woman who did all things well.

'She fascinated every betrousered human around her. She had me—and I don't mind confessing it—she had me to heel along with the rest. Young puppies and old grey dogs who ought to have known better—oh, they all came up and crawled round her skirts and whined and fawned when she whistled. They were all guilty, from young Ardmore, a pink cherub of nineteen, outward bound for some clerkship in the consular service, to old Captain Bentley, grizzled and seaworn, and as emotional, to look at, as a Chinese joss. There was a nice middle-aged chap, Perkins, I believe, who forgot his wife was on board until Miss Caruthers sent him to the right-about and back where he belonged.

'Men were wax in her hands. She melted them, or softly moulded them, or incinerated them, as she pleased. There wasn't a steward, even, grand and remote as she was, who at her bidding would have hesitated to souse the Old Man himself with a plate of soup. You have all seen such women—a sort of world's desire to all men. As a man-conqueror she was supreme. She was a whiplash, a sting and a flame, an electric spark. Oh, believe me, at times there were flashes of will that scorched through her beauty and seduction and smote a victim into blank and shivering idiocy and fear!

'And don't fail to mark, in the light of what is to come, that she was a prideful woman: pride of race, pride of caste, pride of sex, pride of power—she had it all, a pride strange and wilful and terrible.

'She ran the ship, she ran the voyage, she ran everything—and she ran Dennitson. That he had outdistanced the pack even the least wise of us admitted. That she liked him, and that this feeling was growing, there was not a doubt. I am certain that she looked on him with kinder eyes than she had ever looked with on man before. We still worshipped and were always hanging about waiting to be whistled up, though we knew that Dennitson was laps and laps ahead of us. What might have happened we shall never know, for we came to Colombo and something else happened.

'You know Colombo, and how the native boys dive for coins in the shark-infested bay? Of course it is only among the ground sharks and fish sharks that they venture. It is almost uncanny the way they know sharks and can sense the presence of a real killer—a tiger shark, for instance, or a grey nurse strayed up from

Australian waters. But let such a shark appear and, long before the passengers can guess, every mother's son of them is out of the water in a wild scramble for safety.

'It was just after tiffin and Miss Caruthers was holding her usual court under the deck-awnings. Old Captain Bentley had just been whistled up and had granted her what he had never granted before—nor since—permission for the boys to come up on the promenade deck. You see, Miss Caruthers was a swimmer and she was interested. She took up a collection of all our small change and herself tossed it overside, singly and in handfuls, arranging the terms of the contests, chiding a miss, giving extra rewards to clever wins; in short, managing the whole exhibition.

'She was especially keen on their jumping. You know, jumping feet-first from a height, it is very difficult to hold the body perpendicularly while in the air. The centre of gravity of the human body is high, and the tendency is to overtopple, but the little beggars employed a method new to her, which she desired to learn. Leaping from the davits of the boat deck above, they plunged downward, their faces and shoulders bowed forward, looking at the water; and only at the last moment did they abruptly straighten up and enter the water erect and true.

'It was a pretty sight. Their diving was not so good, though there was one of them who was excellent at it, as he was at all the other stunts. Some white man must have taught him, for he made the proper swan dive and did it as beautifully as I have ever seen it done. You know, it is head-first into the water; and from a great height the problem is to enter the water at the perfect angle. Miss the angle and it means at the least a twisted back and injury for life. Also, it has meant death for many a bungler. This boy could do it—seventy feet I know he cleared in one dive from the rigging—clenched hands on chest, head thrown back, sailing more like a bird, upward and out, and out and down, body flat on the air, so that if it struck the surface in that position it would be split in half like a herring. But the moment before the water is reached the head drops forward, the hands go out and lock the arms in an arch in advance of the head, and the body curves gracefully downward and enters the water just right.

This the boy did again and again to the delight of all of us, but particularly of Miss Caruthers. He could not have been a moment over twelve or thirteen, yet he was by far the cleverest of the gang. He was the favourite of his crowd and its leader. Though there were many older than he, they acknowledged his chieftaincy. He was a beautiful boy, a lithe young god in breathing bronze, eyes wide apart, intelligent and daring—a bubble, a mote, a beautiful flash and sparkle of life. You have seen wonderfully glorious creatures—animals, anything, a leopard, a horse—restless, eager, too much alive ever to be still, silken of muscle, each slightest movement a benediction of grace, every action wild, untrammelled, and over all spilling out that intense vitality, that sheen and lustre of living light. The boy had it. Life poured out of him almost in an effulgence. His skin glowed with it. It burned in his eyes. I swear I could almost hear it crackle from him. Looking at him, it was as if a whiff of ozone came to one's nostrils—so fresh and young was he, so resplendent with health, so wildly wild.

'This was the boy, and it was he who gave the alarm in the midst of the sport. The boys made a dash of it for the gangway platform, swimming the fastest strokes they knew, pell-mell, floundering and splashing, fright in their faces, clambering out with jumps and surges, any way to get out, lending one another a hand to safety, till all were strung along the gangway and peering down into the water.

' "What is the matter?" asked Miss Caruthers.

' "A shark, I fancy," Captain Bentley answered. "Lucky little beggars that he didn't get one of them."

' "Are they afraid of sharks?" she asked.

' "Aren't you?" he asked back.

'She shuddered, looked overside at the water and made a *moue*.

' "Not for the world would I venture where a shark might be," she said, and shuddered again. "They are horrible! Horrible!"

'The boys came up on the promenade deck, clustering close to the rail and worshipping Miss Caruthers, who had flung them such a wealth of bakshish. The performance being over, Captain Bentley motioned to them to clear out; but she stopped him.

' "One moment, please, Captain. I have always understood that the natives are not afraid of sharks."

'She beckoned the boy of the swan dive nearer to her and signed to him to dive over again. He shook his head and, along with all his crew behind him, laughed as if it were a good joke.

' "Shark," he volunteered, pointing to the water.

' "No!" she said. "There is no shark."

'But he nodded his head positively and the boys behind him nodded with equal positiveness.

' "No, no, no!" she cried. And then to us: "Who'll lend me a half-crown and a sovereign?"'

'Immediately the half-dozen of us were presenting her with half-crowns and sovereigns, and she accepted the two coins from young Ardmore.

'She held up the half-crown for the boys to see, but there was no eager rush to the rail preparatory to leaping. They stood there grinning sheepishly. She offered the coin to each one individually, and each, as his turn came, rubbed his foot against his calf, shook his head and grinned. Then she tossed the half-crown overboard. With wistful, regretful faces they watched its silver flight through the air, but not one moved to follow it.

' "Don't do it with the sovereign," Dennitson said to her in a low voice.

'She took no notice, but held up the gold coin before the eyes of the boy of the swan dive.

' "Don't!" said Captain Bentley. "I wouldn't throw a sick cat overside with a shark around."

'But she laughed, bent on her purpose, and continued to dazzle the boy.

' "Don't tempt him," Dennitson urged. "It is a fortune to him and he might go over after it."

' "Wouldn't you?" she flared at him. "If I threw it?" This last more softly.

'Dennitson shook his head.

' "Your price is high," she said. "For how many sovereigns would you go?"

' "There are not enough coined to get me overside," was his answer.

'She debated a moment, the boy forgotten in her tilt with Dennitson.

' "For me?" she said very softly.

' "To save your life—yes; but not otherwise."

'She turned back to the boy. Again she held the coin before his eyes, dazzling him with the vastness of its value. Then she made as if to toss it out, and involuntarily he made a half movement towards the rail, but was checked by sharp cries of reproof from his companions. There was anger in their voices as well.

' "I know it is only fooling." Dennitson said. "Carry it as far as you like, but for Heaven's sake don't throw it."

'Whether it was that strange wilfulness of hers, or whether she doubted the boy could be persuaded, there is no telling. It was unexpected to all of us. Out from the shade of the awning the coin flashed golden in the blaze of sunshine and fell towards the sea in a glittering arch. Before a hand could stay him the boy was over the rail and curving beautifully downward after the coin. Both were in the air at the same time. It was a pretty sight. The sovereign cut the water sharply, and at the very spot, almost at the same instant with scarcely a splash, the boy entered.

'From the quicker-eyed black boys watching came an exclamation. We were all at the rail. Don't tell me it is necessary for a shark to turn on its back. That one didn't. In the clear water, from the height we were above it, we saw everything. The shark was a big brute and with one drive he cut the boy squarely in half.

'There was a murmur or something from among us—who made it I did not know; it might have been I. And then there was silence. Miss Caruthers was the first to speak. Her face was deathly white.

' "I—I never dreamed!" she said, and laughed a short, hysterical laugh.

'All her pride was at work to give her control. She turned weakly towards Dennitson, and then on from one to another of us. In her eyes was a terrible sickness and her lips were trembling. We were brutes—oh, I know it, now that I look back upon it; but we did nothing!

' "Mr Dennitson," she said—"Tom, won't you take me below?"

'He never changed the direction of his gaze, which was the bleakest I have ever seen in a man's face; nor did he move an eyelid. He took a cigarette from his case and lighted it. Captain Bentley made a nasty sound in his throat and spat overboard. That was all—that and the silence.

'She turned away and started to walk firmly down the deck. Twenty feet away she swayed and thrust a hand against the wall to save herself; and so she went on, supporting herself against the cabins and walking very slowly.'

Treloar ceased. He turned his head and favoured the little man with a look of cold inquiry. 'Well?' he said finally. 'Classify her.'

The little man gulped and swallowed.

'I have nothing to say,' he said. 'Nothing whatever to say.'

The Better Part of Valour

This was the sixth year that Mrs Lambert and the Major had gone on holiday together. They had first met on a coach tour of Scotland; the Major, always nimble at getting aboard before anyone else, had chivalrously given her his own window-seat when, the couples having possessed the double seats, the single passengers came bumping along the aisle seeking a haven. Thereafter he had always kept the window-seat for her, and stowed her raincoat up on the rack with his own. Thus they became a couple, with a couple's advantages. And, self-sufficient though Mrs Lambert was, these were not negligible.

They found they both lived in south London, Mrs Lambert in Wimbledon, the Major in what he called his bachelor pad in Putney. Six weeks after their return from Scotland the Major invited her to be his lady at his regimental dinner-dance held annually at the Connaught Rooms. Mrs Lambert consented; and six weeks later invited him to partner her at her local bridge club. He was not a good player and she did not ask him again; but the pattern was formed, and once a month or so he would invite her to a theatre and she would invite him to supper at her house, other people being present to make up a four.

It seemed natural that the following year they should repeat the holiday arrangement. This time they decided on a coach tour of the châteaux of the Loire, and very enjoyable it was. The next year it was Holland, the bulb fields allied to Franz Hals and the Rijksmuseum. Then came the Rhine, rather disappointing ('The Rhine maidens must have choked to death years ago,' observed Mrs Lambert); then Treasures of Italy, by air to Nice and thence a coach to Milan, Florence and Sienna. Exhausting, but with two of you so much easier and so very much worth while.

This year it was Greece.

They always made their own separate bookings. That way there was no embarrassment, financial or otherwise. Besides, the Major was apt to be a little slapdash, to take what the travel agents said on trust and not check times or schedules. As a soldier he expected

his orders to be carried out and took an airy view of making sure—
'It's those fellers' job,' he said. 'They ought to know.' But Mrs Lambert always made sure and sometimes saved the Major if not from disaster at least dismay. 'Chappie hadn't got me a reservation,' he'd say. 'Damned inefficient, but it's okay now.'

Mrs Lambert's accommodation was always slightly more expensive than the Major's, with a bathroom and a better view. 'I can doss down any old where,' he said, 'so long as the grub's up to scratch.' He was full of boyish gusto about food and drink, but in fact had a more delicate digestion than Mrs Lambert who, in her quiet way, consumed everything. But neither of them cared for alcohol, which spared them the embarrassment of who should pay for the drinks. Tips she allowed the Major to take care of— that, and luggage, was one of the advantages of travelling with a man. But on the rare occasions when they needed a taxi or an excursion not on the itinerary she insisted that she paid. 'You wouldn't be doing this but for me,' she'd say. 'You must allow me to treat myself to a small extravagance.' He would yield, but tip the driver with a prodigal air. Mrs Lambert suspected he had only his pension.

Whereas she had four houses in Raynes Park, six in Wandsworth, and the one she lived in, a semi-detached, semi-timbered 1920s-ish villa in what had been an almost country lane when she and John Lambert married in the 1930s. She had remained there after he died; the house suited her, although of course she did not need three bedrooms, having no children. An agent managed her properties but in fact she kept a close watch on everything, deciding when to sell and when to buy, when to redecorate or convert or seek planning permission for an added amenity. She understood perfectly every aspect of the various Rent Acts and of Capital Gains, although her agent did not know this.

Nor did the Major. The Major knew nothing about her circumstances save that she had been a widow for some twenty-five years and owned her own house. He would never ask and she would never tell him, for although over the six years of their companionship they had grown closer they had not grown more intimate.

True, their meetings were now once a month or even every three weeks; and, true, she no longer always arranged that other people should be present when he came to supper. Often it was just the two of them, a simple meal and the lemon barley water she kept specially for him, and watching television afterwards. As he put on his coat and set off to walk first up, then down the hill to Putney

('Never use transport if Shanks's mare can take you,' he said, but perhaps it was partly to save fares) he often looked wistful; and latterly he had taken to holding her hand as they stood at the open front door, looking into her face with his bright blue eyes, and sighing. Once or twice he had even kissed her hand, blushed, jammed his tweed hat on his head and bolted down the path. No reference was ever made to these occasions. She behaved as though they had not happened, although the place where his moustache had pressed seemed to stay hot and moist for several moments.

She knew that at the slightest relaxation of her habitual neutrality something might burst from him. She had known this for quite a long time. He would dare nothing without a sign from her. Somewhat to her surprise, she had lately begun to consider giving that sign.

The coach party spent their first night in a noisy hotel off Omonia Square. As was his custom, the Major made it clear at Reception and to the hotel lobby in general that his room was on the fourth floor while that of Mrs Lambert was on the first, which came as a surprise to other members of the party who had assumed, since they had travelled self-sufficiently together from London, that this round, bald man and his neat companion were man and wife.

The party consisted of what at first glance appeared to be the identical people who had been on all the other coach trips back over the years: the elderly couples; the pairs of middle-aged female friends; the several younger or older single women; the three single men, two old and widowed, one youngish and lissome. Everything had gone smoothly so far, except that two singles had been booked into a double, and a tartan hold-all belonging to a large single lady was missing. While search was made its owner, Miss Fordyce, stood lamenting in the middle of the lobby, her hair in wisps, her cardigan slipping from her uneven shoulders. The bag was found still in the coach, and everyone began to edge hopefully towards the lift.

Before they could disperse, however, there came the sound of several sharp handclaps and a harsh voice crying, 'If you please—attention!' A small, black-clothed woman, her head wrapped in a paisley turban which made her face seem larger and more yellow even than it was, made an imperious gesture. 'You—Partos Tours—come, come, here to me!' she cried.

They came. She surveyed them with eyes narrow and glistening as black olives, set close on either side of a long camel's nose. She smiled, fearsomely. 'So. That is good. You come when I say. That is how it shall be, yes? From today till you leave Greece, yes? I call, you come. So.'

She regarded with satisfaction their stupefied faces. 'So. I know you but you don't know me, yes? I am Madame Aphrodite Mavrodopoulos and I am your guide. From now until you leave my country I tell you everything, take you everywhere, yes? You don't do one thing without I tell you except when you have special free time for visit shops, buy beautiful things. I tell you where. So. Soon I know all your names. Very quickly I learn all about you. And you learn all about me, yes? My name difficult for English people so you call me Madame Aphrodite, yes? You learn too that when I say Come, you come, quick, quick. If naughty boys and girls don't come when I say, they get left behind, yes?'

She smiled wolfishly, looking round the circle of faces and giving a little nod. 'So. Now to your rooms and then dinner, then as you please. But tomorrow. . . .' She raised a terrible sun-baked hand. 'Tomorrow down here, all, at nine o'clock, yes? Not nine one minute, nine five minutes, but nine exact. Otherwise you get left behind. Tomorrow nine o'clock here, for visit Acropolis, Philopappus, Agora. Return hotel one o'clock, lunch and siesta. Four o'clock exact, coach for Daphni, Eleusis and Piraeus. Next day, we start on tour. Eight o'clock exact leave for Peloponnesus. So. Small luggage, yes? No forgettings. Ten days before we get back here. Now we say night-night until tomorrow. Nine o'clock exact and no silly shoes, please, or you break your legs. So. Sweet dreams.' She turned, an immense black handbag knocking at her bony hip, and spun through the revolving doors.

The coach party looked at each other. ''Ware minefields,' muttered the Major.

In another time and place Madame Aphrodite could have been a galley-master, standing astride the gangway on either side of which, day after sweltering day, her captives cringed in their allotted places. Over their bent heads her gaze swept like a lash, checking, identifying, while instead of the time-giver's drum her voice rasped out over the microphone a ceaseless flow of instruction.

For Madame Aphrodite (Madame Aspro, the Major called her after the second day, but not in her hearing) was extremely efficient. Not only did even hotel receptionists bend before her but she absolutely knew her Classical stuff. The glory of being Greek had consumed her, shrivelled her up, so that now, in old age (and who knew how old she could be, any more than Medusa, clambering up and down the slippery paving-stones, the ancient scree, an umbrella over her turbaned head, her yellow face dry as a lizard while all those behind her sweated, sweated), it no longer illumined her with the rich, life-enhancing glow of an eternal flame but had seared her into a bitter, knotty brand which smoked and sparked and made the eyes water.

She knew everything, everything; and behind the facts she knew the spirit, the truth that had spread and fertilized and made the world beautiful so that always, for ever, mankind was in its debt. She knew the absolute truth, and the truth was herself; yet day after day from April to October, in her old age (how old, Medusa?), if she were lucky and resourceful, she must lay this truth out before coachloads of insensitive non-Greeks, must tell them facts and get them fed, make toilet stops and stops to buy souvenirs, must count them in and out of this shrine of majesty and that, see their eyes glaze at pillars, cloisters, Pantocrators, hear them whisper of heat or their bowels or the moussaka at that last place while she poured out on them the splendour of the Mysteries or of Marathon. The fury and frustration made her voice harsh and her eyes hard as she drove them sheep-like to and fro, telling them things they did not hear, showing them things they would not see. She knew everything, everything, and all they wanted were schoolroom facts and the time they'd be stopping for lunch.

She had a certain inbred respect for men, so the married couples and the three bachelors were more or less safe from her, although the lissome youngish man fared badly once or twice. But with the unattached women she was pitiless. Sarcastic comments about beauty sleep were made if they were late for the morning departures; and, if they strayed from the main party during the day, 'You have a boyfriend in the olive grove, yes? No use to look for the chauffeur, he has a wife and five children.' They smiled weakly and pretended it was a joke.

But the worst butt of all was that Miss Fordyce who had mislaid her tartan holdall on arrival in Omonia Square. Not only was Miss Fordyce magnetic to ill fortune but she contributed to it herself. That it should be her room that was over the kitchens or her wash-basin which regurgitated someone else's scummy water was bad luck, but that she should leave her cardigan in the arena at the very top of the ruins at Delphi or drop her sunglasses down the granite terraces of Epidaurus was her own fault. She should have known better than to eat that extremely greasy goat meat on the way to Olympia, certainly better than to insist that she was secure for the excursion next morning.

It was she who got lost in Nauplia (how can one lose one's way in Nauplia, for heaven's sake?) and who fell into a small crevasse at Corinth, spraining a wrist. Everyone agreed that Miss Fordyce was very game; and everyone wished that she were not in their party.

As the Major said, there is one on every trip but with any luck they may be pretty or young or amusing and so their sins are forgiven them most of the time. Miss Fordyce was none of these things, but a big, lumpy, elderly woman with weak ankles, the result of a childhood illness that had nearly carried her off, as she told everyone several times, especially when her slowness in getting in or out of anything held up everyone else. 'Miss Fordyce, please to wait till the last so we don't lose too much time, yes?... Miss Fordyce, please to go to the coach now so we don't get waiting.... Miss Fordyce, so often I tell you hold your feet in so we don't all fall over them, yes?' The nagging was incessant, and everyone else looked out of the windows or fussed with hand luggage.

As the most noticeably masculine man among them (for somehow marriage seemed to neutralize the husbands of the couples) the Major carried a certain weight, and Madame Aphrodite treated him with a fearsome archness. 'Ah, Major, come come come! Be so kind as to order coffees while I see that the WCs are not locked.'

'Wilco,' would answer the Major, deftly steering Mrs Lambert to the most comfortable seat, then making sure they both got the first service.

Sometimes Madame Aphrodite sat at their table, watching derisively as they emptied the powdered coffee into their cups, her long nose inhaling the aroma of her own Greek brew (Greek, not Turkish, yes?). Mrs Lambert sat very composedly on these occasions, knowing that Madame Aphrodite's glittering speculation was upon her, wondering what and why. She of all people knew how far apart at every hotel were Mrs Lambert's room and that of the Major.

The Major handled these coffee breaks with nervous gallantry, his face redder than ever, his blue eyes uneasy, a small boy at tea with Matron. Mrs Lambert admired him; she knew he was frightened of Madame Aphrodite, as were they all—except, probably, herself. As she had never, since she was a girl, felt herself inferior to anyone, Mrs Lambert had no reason to fear anything. But she was glad that the presence of the Major shielded her from Madame Aphrodite's lash.

Miss Fordyce, flopping and gasping under it, turned hither and thither for help. Sometimes she was allowed to take cover with a couple, married or female; but not for long because, ignoble though everyone knew it to be, they none of them wanted to be bothered with the poor creature. She was a bore; and, just as Madame Aphrodite implied, she was also a nuisance, delaying, irritating, trailing behind.

She turned to the Major; and he, kind-hearted and in some ways naïve as he was, treated her gently. He listened to the story of her childhood illness; of her father who had been a noted archaeologist, which was why she had come to Greece; of her two cats and their quaint ways; of the literary circle of which she was the secretary, and the humdrum subjects of their meetings. She told him about the bad rooms, the bad food, the bad seats, the bad manners which, quite correctly, she felt she received wherever she went. But she did not dare to complain about Madame Aphrodite. Her fear and shame were too great.

The Major listened, sometimes humming under his breath. His gaze would wander to Mrs Lambert and they would exchange a small, smiling look. He had not much idea of how to extricate himself from Miss Fordyce, beyond looking at his watch and exclaiming, 'I say, just look at the time!' or, if he saw her approaching soon enough, turning his back and moving Mrs Lambert hastily away, as though they had not noticed her. Soon Mrs Lambert began to abet him in this. She was sorry for Miss Fordyce for, before she met the Major, she had herself suffered many of the penalties of a middle-aged woman travelling alone. But she had never been so incompetent, so tiresome as Miss Fordyce. Besides, it was she who had the Major.

As they sat in their accustomed places in the coach Mrs Lambert thought seriously about the Major. The tour was almost over; they were on their way back to Athens, where tomorrow they would have a morning shopping and, when the heat of the day subsided, visit Sounion to watch the sunset from the temple of Poseidon on the cliff. The next day back to England. And then what?

For Mrs Lambert knew that things could not remain exactly as they had been. You cannot, no matter how it seems, both have your cake and eat it. She had had the cake for six years; had the time come when she should eat it? His wistful looks, the occasional kissed hand, had all been signals that a slow swell was mounting. During the past ten days he had been noticeably tender; beyond the normal call of good manners he had cherished her in numberless little ways. The last few evenings, as the coach had neared its overnight stop, or after dinner, walking in the soft air beside the café tables, he had taken her hand and she had let him. Not during the daytime when anyone could see, but in the darkness of the coach or among the dusty oleanders of a little square. He had breathed heavily but said nothing; he did not dare, for although he had her hand she gave no sign that she was aware of it. Her gaze remained friendly but cool as it had always been, her voice calm. Thus she was when checking her income-tax assessment or acquiring a new property.

But Mrs Lambert knew that soon she must make up her mind. She did not actually want to, but as a businesswoman she recognized that there is a time to buy and a time to sell, a time to make an offer and to receive one. By the time they returned to England she would have decided whether to marry the Major.

They saw the tiny ivory bones of the temple, standing high between the cobalt sky and the turquoise sea, long before they reached it. The heat of the day was declining and this, the last expedition of the tour, had an end-of-term air about it. This time tomorrow they would all be back at home again, reading the accumulated mail, watering the plants, drinking a decent cup of tea. They had enjoyed it all, of course; and the colour films which they would finish up now at Sounion would be despatched to the developers' first thing. But, as their coach drew in beside the others already parked there, they gathered themselves together more sluggishly, followed more slowly up the steep slope on which, still and golden against the cooling sky, the pillars awaited them, and heard with equanimity, for it was the last time, the leather-palmed clap-clap-clap, the leather-throated Come-come-come as Madame Aphrodite clambered on to a broken pediment and forced their attention.

For her too it was the end of term and she could hardly endure them a moment longer. Their lethargic assemblage, their wandering looks infuriated her and only by the exercise of greatest self-discipline could she summon them under her in their proper obedient knot to assert her own harsh commentary against the rivalling French and German groups who, with their own shrill guides, already milled and wallowed over the sacred stones.

'Come come come! Partos people, please to come here. Please

to keep close for listening. Never mind looking now, now you listen, yes? Come come come!' She could hardly wait to be done with them, to deliver this last harangue into their bovine faces, to let them clamber about and take their silly snapshots and then shoo them back down the hill, into the coach, back to the city and out out out into oblivion, never to be seen again. She would accept their tips, crushing the notes into her big black handbag to count when she reached the haven of her own two rooms in a peeling house behind the University. Gnarled feet bare on the tiled floor, she would push open the shutters that had kept out the heat all day and breathe in the solitude, the peace of the tour's end. She would speak to no one for two whole days. She would forget these Partos people utterly, expunge them, folding their tips into the old cashbox against her older age. Deny that, next Monday evening, there would be another lot to start with all over again.

Raising her voice, she crammed the final dose of information into their inattentive ears. Above the babel of the rival groups the columns breathed silence, the luminous sky darkening into the sea, the sun sliding down towards the headland where soon lights would come on and a new round of life begin in the seaside suburbs of the city. Far below the cliff where they swarmed at the feet of the temple two fishing boats passed like feathers across the rippled sea, and suddenly Madame Aphrodite could do no more.

'So. That is enough, yes? Now you must look for yourselves. Ten minutes only, then back quick quick to the coach. No waiting. Ten minutes only.' She climbed down and, turning her back on her party, pushed through the other groups and out of sight.

'Well,' said the Major, 'she cut that jolly short.' He took Mrs Lambert's elbow and helped her across the broken pavement to the cliff's edge and the sunset. 'Can't say I'll be sorry to see the last of the old girl. Bit of a battle-axe, eh? Still, knows her stuff.'

They stood and looked at the sunset, moving aside so as not to occlude the view of various photographers jockeying for space and angles. Two huge Germans crashed past them. His grip on her arm tightened. 'Wine-dark sea, eh? Can never quite see it, myself. But beautiful, beautiful. Something we'll never forget. I never will, anyway. Treasured memory—like so many, eh? Marjorie. . . .'

She moved away. Not here, with German and French and American clamorous about them, the scrape of feet, the click of cameras. She climbed up on to the temple floor and he hurried after her. 'Here, let me give you a hand.'

'Thank you.'

A large form swooped and clutched. 'Oh, Mrs Lambert, Major—do come! I've found it. I knew it was here because Father always maintained it was a fake. It wasn't at all his period, of course, but to me it has always been an ambition, to actually *see*. . . . Do come.' Miss Fordyce, flushed, her cardigan slipping off her shoulders as usual, drew them with her to the landward side of the temple, stumbling over the pavings to one of the grooved columns. 'There—see? It really is! Think of it, imagine it! Him standing there, frowning perhaps, his hair blowing, carving away. . . . What a thing to do! Vandalism, of course, but still. . . . There it is!' She reached forward and let her fingers trace the letters carved into the stone. 'Byron!'

'Byron?'

'Lord Byron. She should have told us, for you'd easily miss it if you didn't know it was here. Imagine!' Her face was radiant, grey hair falling into her eyes. 'Do look. Do you see it?'

Mrs Lambert and the Major moved forward and Miss Fordyce stepped back. Her foot slid and she fell awkwardly with a small shriek. Several people nearby turned their heads but the Major was bending over her.

'Oh dear,' she gasped. 'Oh dear. How silly of me.'

'Are you hurt?'

'No. No, I don't think so.' They helped her to her feet. 'Oh dear. Wicked Lord Byron!' She smiled but her face was pale. Mrs Lambert picked up her cardigan and put it round her. 'Oh dear, what a silly thing! I think perhaps I'll go back to the coach. These places are dreadfully dangerous, really they ought to warn you.'

'Let me help you.' The Major took her arm.

'Well, thank you—just down the hill. These stones, so treacherous. But we did see Byron. . . .'

Mrs Lambert watched them make their cautious way down the eroded hillside and disappear between the ranked bodies of the charabancs, pale now in the falling dusk. Some of the other groups had already left but a number of people still crawled about the temple, destroying the evening peace, and Mrs Lambert wondered what it would be like to see it alone and silent, whether the ghosts of those who had worshipped here would steal out, as the stored heat did, from the stones. She let her fingers move as Miss Fordyce's had over the flowing letters incised in the column, arrogant and elegant: Byron. She never read poetry, but just the same. . . .

The Major had returned. 'Poor old thing—it would be her it happened to, eh?'

'Is she all right?'

'Perfectly. The coach was locked, no sign of the driver chappie, so I sat her down on the grass beside it and told her to wait. Madame Aspro'll be after us all in a moment anyway.'

Sure enough, soon they heard the clap clap clap of Madame Aphrodite, emerged from some hidden crevice of the cliff, and joined the others moving down the hillside to the parking-place. Madame Aphrodite came behind them, a testy sheepdog. It was almost dark now, suddenly. The driver was in his seat, the coach already pulsating. Everyone clambered in quickly, eager now for it all to be over. Madame Aphrodite climbed in last, surveyed them neatly packed in their double seats, counting under her breath.

Her face froze. 'There is one missing,' she grated. 'Who, please, is missing?'

A hush fell. Each looked guiltily at his neighbour, thanking God they were in their place. The driver revved the engine.

'Who, please, is missing?' Her voice was like a saw.

A whispered hiss went round the seats: Fordyce, Miss Fordyce, Fordyce. . . .

'So. Miss Fordyce.' Madame Aphrodite folded her yellow arms in menacing satisfaction. 'Always Miss Fordyce. Someone has seen Miss Fordyce, yes?' No one spoke. 'Miss Fordyce has perhaps fallen from the cliff? She has taken a taxi home? We are already ten minutes late and Andros here is needing his supper. Who knows of Miss Fordyce?'

Not a sound.

Mrs Lambert turned and looked at the Major. His face was flushed and he was staring at the back of the seat in front of him.

The driver let out a long blare on his klaxon.

Madame Aphrodite's yellow grew pale. Her eyes seemed to send out sparks of fury and she banged her handbag down on the hard little folding seat on which she had to travel.

'One more minute only we wait! Who has seen Miss Fordyce?'

The Major got to his feet. 'I'll go and look for her,' he muttered. The driver issued another terrible blast from his horn and revved the engine even more.

At the Major's movement everyone began to chatter: Just like her, always the same, silly old fool, lack of consideration, dead tired, want to get back and rest, some people never learn. . . .

He bumbled his way down the aisle, Madame Aphrodite a knot of fury by the door. 'Shan't be a tick,' he said, and began to dismount; but as he did so a pale figure loomed out of the dusk and Miss Fordyce, distraught, staggered to the steps.

'Oh, thank goodness, thank goodness! I was afraid you'd have gone....'

The Major drew back. Miss Fordyce was literally wringing her hands, her hair on end, her voice a wail. 'So sorry but not my fault, not my fault at all. It was the wrong bus. I was waiting by the wrong bus.'

As she began to haul herself aboard the Major turned and retreated down the aisle. He looked neither to left nor right.

Madame Aphrodite's voice cut like a saw. 'So. The wrong bus.'

'Yes, quite the wrong bus. It was locked, you see, so I didn't notice. I just waited there....'

'You didn't notice. In ten days you don't notice the colour of the coach? You don't notice the name Partos written big, big on the sides? Do you notice more perhaps the colour of the driver's eyes?'

Miss Fordyce stood in the doorway staring in terror at Madame Aphrodite, whose small frame seemed to vibrate.

'You don't hear me say ten minutes only, you don't see us return down the path, you don't see us get in the coach marked Partos? You don't stay with everyone as I tell you always? You are dreaming perhaps of a rendezvous with Poseidon? You are a sea nymph, yes?'

'Oh!' Miss Fordyce went white, then a mottled raspberry. 'How dare you....'

'Get to your seat and let us have no more silly argument!' Madame Aphrodite snatched up her handbag from the hard little seat and plumped herself down in it, snarling over her shoulder, 'There is always one who is trouble to all the rest. I thank God my hands are now washed of you.'

Miss Fordyce stumbled to her seat, past the prim knees of the widower who had got landed with her at the beginning of the tour and who now clicked his knuckles nervously and stared straight ahead. With a lurch and a roar the coach began to move and was soon hastening, at well over the normal speed, back towards Athens.

It was quite dark now. On the one side lay the hills with their low trees and the villas of diplomats and rich Athenians pale among their greenery; on the other the sea, silent and calm as the night, lapping secretly along the shore. Sooner than seemed possible they reached the wide new road through the suburbs, edged by cafés and hotels, brightly lit and loud with music and traffic. Then away from the sea, back up the airport highway, past the dry earth and desiccated buildings, back into the narrow turmoil, the heat, the lights, the crowded streets and cafés and, glimpsed now and then floating high above the roofs against the night sky, the tiny floodlit stillness of the Parthenon.

They reached the hotel. They gathered their belongings, edged down the aisle, climbed out. No one had spoken during the whole journey back, and even now they could not. Madame Aphrodite stood on the pavement, hunched and silent. Not looking at her, they shook her gnarled hand with mumbled thanks, leaving within it the notes on which they had decided earlier in the day. Silently she stuffed them into her bag, her long-nosed face impassive, her eyes remote. Only Miss Fordyce, tear-blotched and dishevelled, did not pause beside her but hurried past into the hotel and up into her room (next to the service lift), not to be seen again until next morning in the airport bus. She sat alone and spoke to no one, all the way back to Cromwell Road. And perhaps beyond.

The Major and Mrs Lambert spoke. At dinner they spoke about the menu, about the menus over the past ten days, about the places they had stayed and the objects they had bought; and they shared their conversation with several other members of the party, comparing notes and being promised copies of the photographs which all hoped would turn out satisfactory. Mrs Lambert excused herself from the Major's suggestion of a last turn together in Syntagma Square and went up to her room. Like Miss Fordyce, she did not appear until the airport bus was due; when the Major tapped on her door to see why she was not at breakfast she answered, without opening it, that a tray had been sent up and that she had not finished packing.

She let him queue for her at the Duty Free shop, and accepted quietly the bottle of perfume he brought her as a gift. She did not speak much on the flight but closed her eyes and kept her hands in her lap.

He retrieved their suitcases at Heathrow and carried them to the bus, paid their fares (nice to handle proper money again) and at Cromwell Road got a taxi.

She agreed that London looked dirty but that everything, as they neared Putney and his flat, looked nice and green; that it was good to be home again no matter what strikes and inflation might await them. When he fell silent, pursing his lips and glancing at her nervously out of the corners of his eyes, she said at last: 'How much did you tip Madame Aphrodite?'

'Madame Aspro?' He was alarmed. 'Haven't a clue, not now.'

'You must have some idea.' She opened her handbag and took out her purse.

'Oh—well, three hundred drachs, something like that. But really, I don't want ... I mean, no need. ...'

She made a silent calculation, then put the right amount into his hand. He tried to give it back. 'Honestly, I don't want. ... That's always been my pigeon.'

'Please,' she said, her manner tranquil, 'I would rather take my share of Madame Aphrodite.'

He looked at her and she looked back. His round red face turned slowly redder still and he glanced away, fumbling the money into his pocket. 'Well, if you insist.'

'Yes,' she said.

They reached his block of flats and he got out. On the pavement he stood, his luggage beside him, bald head shining, gazing in.

'Marjorie ...,' he said.

She leaned forward and swung the taxi door shut between them. 'Some other time,' she said.

The following year Mrs Lambert spent her holiday with her sister-in-law at Sidmouth. And the year after that.

She did not miss the Major.

The Long-Distance Train

At that time the Tudor Green station-master was a Mr Read. Not long since promoted to this position, he seemed a rather insignificant although businesslike sort of person, but internally he often suffered with acuteness even while outwardly calm.

Perhaps conscious of his own essential incompetence, he was always wondering how he had risen so high and always fearing a fall. He dreaded making mistakes. Sometimes he woke all cold with fear in the middle of the night, and lay quaking beside his young wife after a dream of a terrible railway accident that had been caused by him.

'Anything wrong?' murmured Mrs Read, roused by his restless movements.

'No, dear, nothing. Go to sleep again. Sorry I disturbed you.'

As in the case of many successful men, he had often the bitter taste of failure in the midst of his success. He felt the want of solid strength behind the grand external show. He felt it while going his rounds in the early morning. Men were shunting a truck by hand, and he hustled them feebly; then he hurried away, to avoid hearing their grumblings. Hankinson, his chief staff officer, yawned and answered him curtly; and Mr Read for a moment intended to reprove him, and then did not. Instead he left the platform, walked along by the metals past the little gardens of the porters, and went up into the signal cabin. He saw something slightly wrong there, but never spoke of it. He would speak next time.

This often happened—little things about the station not quite as they should be. Or so it seemed to him. A railway station ought to be entirely spick and span, and that is how he wished his station to be. But people did not support him as they should have done. They were careless, not malevolent, he told himself. Want of thought, not want of heart. They wouldn't see, as he did, that an important place like Tudor Green ought to have not only a busy, well-conducted station, but a *popular* station. And he felt, in the whole surrounding atmosphere, that it was not really popular.

Then the authorities told him so. He was summoned to the offices at the great terminus and hauled over the coals about it.

He offered such excuses as he could—hundreds of trains in and out, both electric and steam, none too large a staff, natural impatience of city gentlemen as a race. 'I have a good deal to contend against, sir.' This was a favourite expression of his, and as he used it he rubbed his sandy side whiskers and blinked his mild blue eyes.

They asked him if he was properly served. 'Come, spit it out. If any of your staff are inefficient, say so.'

For a moment then he thought of smashing Hankinson with a word, but the next moment he had a mental vision of fat Mrs Hankinson and the four Hankinson children. Moreover, with the vision there came a queer, unexpected thought that old Hankinson, although stupid, dilatory, and sometimes impudent, was really rather fond of him.

'No, sir. No complaints,' he said stoutly. 'If there's blame, I take it on myself.'

And he went back to Tudor Green rubbing his right-hand whiskers and feeling sad and dejected.

After this he made feeble little efforts to popularize the place without losing the ideal of spick-and-spanness. As, for instance, he procured a large black dog with a slung money-box to go about the platforms wagging its tail and collecting pennies for the railway orphanage; he arranged for the opening of a flower stall as a thing apart and distinct from the fruiterer's shop; and at Christmas he persuaded the people of W. H. Smith and Son to decorate all three bookstalls with holly and coloured paper.

Not only for meals but during spare minutes he used to run up into the station-master's house—a sham Gothic erection that dominated the whole station—and cheer his wife by telling her the station news. Thus, towards noon on a foggy March morning, he opened their sitting-room door and saw her seated near the window with her hands folded in her lap in the listless, almost forlorn attitude that of late had become habitual with her.

'Well, how's the world treating you?' she asked, turning her head languidly.

She was a dark-haired, and unquestionably pretty woman of about twenty-eight; and when he first saw her, a hundred miles from here, she had a glowing bright complexion, with eyes that seemed to have flames of health in them, but now her cheeks were pale and the flash of her glance had gone. Looking at her he felt an inward stab of discomfort, if not actual pain, as he thought that perhaps, after all, the air of Tudor Green and the Thames Valley did not really suit her.

'Well,' he said cheeringly, 'we had a little unpleasantness just now. Yes, Nellie, Berry's clerk gave short change again, and the gentleman was very indignant. But I smoothed him down all right. There'll be no report made.... The girl at Abbot's flower stall has a sore throat, and has wrapped a piece of flannel round it. It's very unsightly.... The eleven-twenty loop was shockingly late. Too bad of them. But of course I knew they had a lot to contend against—fog all along the river, held up at Tide End crossover, and a horse box put on to them at Staines.... Hark!'

Down below an electric train had come in with its once strange but now well-known clatter, and up here in the living-room it was as though a very slight earthquake had happened. Two cheap and terribly unattractive vases on the mantelshelf were set tinkling by the vibration, and they continued to tinkle while Mr Read went on talking.

'It's the eleven-fifty-seven down! They don't need me for that. Hankinson can—— Oh, by the bye, I thought you were going for a walk with Mrs Hankinson.'

'In this fog? No, thank you.'

'The fog's cleared up. Yes, the fog's cleared up nicely.' Mr Read said this very cheerfully, as if it was a piece of news to make anybody happy. 'The sun'll break through too. I assure you, it's a regular spring day.'

'I'm glad to hear it,' said Mrs Read fretfully. 'I shouldn't have known it otherwise. All the days here seem pretty much the same—and the seasons too, if it comes to that.'

'Ah,' said Mr Read, wincing, but maintaining his cheerful smile, 'you're a country girl, aren't you? And when I say spring you begin to think of the primroses on the banks, or the violets beginning to show themselves in the woods.'

'Oh, don't, *please*.'

'I understand, dear,' said Mr Read gently, and he rubbed his hands together in a deprecating manner. 'The country's a grand place. But you'll admit that the town has some compensations to offer in exchange. All the life and gaiety.'

'All the what?' said Mrs Read.

'Well—I meant, if only the shops.'

'The shops make one gay—don't they?—when you can't ever afford to go in and buy anything.'

Mr Read scratched his chin as a change from his side whiskers.

'I am aware you feel the loneliness,' he said, slowly and dully. 'But that's why I wished you to make friends.' Then he resumed his cheerful aspect. 'Now, look here. I want you to go out straight away, to oblige me. Yes, I want you to, for a particular purpose.' And, pointing to the mantelpiece, he said he wished her at once to buy the porcelain ornament about which they recently had had a discussion.

'I don't want it. It was hateful of me to ask for it.'

'No, not a bit. So natural. Pretty people like you ought to have pretty things about them.' He had brought a leather purse from the inside pocket of his frock coat, and he laid a Treasury note on the table. 'There, run out and buy it. Then you can throw those vases in the dustbin, as you said—or give them as a present to somebody less fortunate than us.'

Having put on his gold-laced cap he was going, but she came to him and kissed him.

'Oh, how good you are to me! Only, take back the money. I don't want the thing—not any more—honour bright.' And, clinging to him, she burst into tears. 'I'm hateful to you—and you're too good to me, oh, much too good.'

'There, there,' said Mr Read huskily, 'don't cry. Nothing to cry about'; and he drew her closer, and himself kissed her. But as he held her in his arms, enfolding her with this intimate embrace, and feeling his heart melt in tenderness and pity, he had a sudden dreadful sensation that, instead of her being his longed-for comrade, his girl that he had wooed and won, his wife, she was a complete stranger. 'It's all right. Let's make the best of things, not the worst.'

'You must forgive me and make allowances,' she sobbed. 'I'm sorry—but I don't know how it is. My spirits are like your trains. They seem to go up and down forty times a day.'

'Nellie, I know well you aren't quite yourself.' Still holding her, he looked at her face anxiously. 'I've noticed the ups and downs. Your health, dear—this last month especially. It has not been what it should be.' And as he said this he flushed and his whole face seemed to lighten. His pale eyes glowed with the brightness of hope. 'D'you think your upsets mean—— Do you think the real reason may be only just what we desire?'

But Mrs Read shook her head negatively, and said it didn't mean that.

They had no children. That was his supreme failure, altogether the worst thing he had to contend against and perhaps because of it or out of it there had come all this paralysing, deadening sense of secret incompetence.

'Ta-ta,' he said. 'Wanted now. That's the twelve-three.'

There was a nearer and rather bigger earthquake in the room. A steam train had come up. Mr Read hurried away.

Their household consisted of three persons, themselves and a stupid but honest old woman called Emma who acted as servant. But, although with a servant to wait upon her, Mrs Read herself worked too. She rose early, went out to do the marketing, and then was active for a few hours, cleaning the rooms, sometimes with wild ardour; cooking a little, preparing the midday meal to be cooked by Emma. And all this time the station was throbbing and shaking beneath her feet; a thousand footsteps sounded in the booking-hall; if she looked out of a window she saw a flat lead-covered roof with fifty yards of platform below it densely thronged with black city toilers all standing there silent, motionless, a white newspaper in hand, as they waited for their train. The train came in, hiding them all, and then left with an empty platform behind it. Three minutes later, if she looked out once more, the platform was full again, apparently with just the same people.

But by about half-past ten the station became quiet, and, moreover, her work was finished. There was no further work to do, unless she made work, invented work. She sat down by the window of the living-room or climbed the stairs and took a survey from the top floor.

And it was then that the fourth dweller in the house made his presence perceptible. This was the dread companion of men and women that we call the Giant Ennui, or Emptiness, or Frustration, as the case may suggest. He took possession of Mrs Read day after day, making her his, using her as he chose, since he recognized her as that easiest of all victims, a wife whose husband cannot satisfy her wants. And between caresses he whispered the most abominably depressing things.

'Is this life, Nellie Read?' said the whisper. 'Or is it death? Was it for this that you forsook fresh air, a laughing brother and sister, jolly rustic friends and admirers? Is it for this that you always lower your eyes or turn your head when men look at you? Was it to help you gain this that God gave you your face, your heart, and your graceful limbs, together with your wonderful, flaming, instinctive certainty that it would be in your power to open the gates of Heaven for anyone you really loved? Twenty-eight years old too, already. And a foggy morning. And those damned blue vases. Oh, dear; oh, dear! I'm sorry for you, Nellie.'

In the view from the upper floor the most prominent features were the clock tower, the peaked roofs of the part of the station they called the junction, whence started the trains for the underground and tube railways, with the glass-screened passenger bridge over what they termed the through lines, but across all this she used to stare at the dull haze that obscured the eastward sky and spoke to her of London itself, vast, mysterious, near at hand, and yet playing as little part in her life as if it had been a city of dreams or a place surmised to exist on another planet.

It was almost impossible to believe in it as multitudinously alive, full of bright faces and high hopes, full of loves, joys, wickednesses. The little electric trains were always running to it and returning from it, restarting another ten-mile journey as soon as they had completed the last one, and these trumpery trains seemed to her like her own thoughts, always going to and fro over the same dull ground and never getting clear away. The so-called through trains merely ran out into the valley, made a loop, and were driven back to the great terminus. These balked, thwarted steam trains were like one's sentimental and romantic ambitions, cut short and brought to nothing by the narrow limits of one's monotonous existence.

But towards the end of March a tremendous event was announced. For the first time in history a long-distance express train was coming through the station. It would start from a Channel port, skirt round London, and go racing away to the north. It would be the longest-distance train in the United Kingdom. It would come up one day and go down the next, three journeys each way for the week, and on the seventh day it would rest.

The station-master came bounding upstairs to tell Mrs Read all about it. His hands were full of the pink railway bills, and he stammered from excitement as he explained how, because of the geographical position and its connecting links with all parts of the metropolis, Tudor Green had been selected as a stopping-place.

'How long will it stop?'

'Two minutes—not a second more. Yes, I shall have to push

her through inside of two minutes. Oh, Nellie dear, this means a great deal to me.'

It was his chance. He recognized it at once. There was an opportunity of impressing himself on the world and solidifying himself with the company. The long-distance train must raise the prestige of the whole place, and with the growing fame of his station he would become famous too. He made great preliminary efforts—efforts that included a letter to the local newspaper.

'As and from March thirty-one,' wrote Mr Read, 'and linking as it does the north and south of our island without change of compartment, this achievement of railway enterprise fires the imagination. . . .'

There was no doubt that it fired the imagination of Mrs Read. She could think and talk of nothing else.

She was on the platform to see its first arrival. Everything had been swept and garnished; porters were lined up like soldiers; Inspector Hankinson, stung to rapid motion by excitement, flitted here and there; her poor little husband, with fresh gold lace on his cap, was marching about or standing in a Napoleonic attitude.

'Stand back there! Stand back!'

No one was standing forward, but all felt the strain.

The gigantic black shining engine towered high above them; the huge coaches glided past with an unbroken scarlet name-board above the windows; the restaurant car glittered like a small Crystal Palace; then the vast overwhelming thing came to rest.

Mrs Read watched and glowed. Four or five people got out of the train. Nobody got into it. A man at a compartment window shouted for a newspaper, and Smith's boy with his tray ran to him.

'Take your seats. Take your seats.' The porters were calling the new words they had learned. Take your seats for Leicester, Nottingham, Sheffield, Leeds, for Durham—for impossibly remote places. It seemed to her that they were crying, 'Take your seats for novelty, for freedom, for paradise.' A whistle, a white cloud of exhaust steam, then the tremendous puffs, each puff like a thud against one's heart, and the train was moving again. It was gliding past her. It had been panting to get away from this dead suburban world, and it seemed to give a long shiver of relief. She shivered too.

She watched it every day, dressing herself for it in her best clothes, as if she were going to church. Those two minutes had more life in them than the whole of the twenty-four hours. They *were* the day.

Sometimes she sat on a bench all the time gazing with ardent eyes, noticing and absorbing every minute detail of its passage. Always, always, there was interest, excitement. Such wonderful people got out of it and changed to the other lines—strong sun-burnt people utterly unlike anæmic residents of the suburb; people with magnificent handbags, aristocrats; people that she knew must be Americans; tall, elegant women with coloured veils and grey male companions in tortoise-shell spectacles; once policemen with a terrible prisoner in handcuffs, a murderer perhaps.

Almost at once she noticed the man in the train, the man who had shouted for a newspaper. He came up on Monday and went down on Saturday every week. He travelled in the Sheffield coach.

For the first two or three times that he looked at her and smiled at her so boldly she lowered her eyes. Then he kissed the tips of his fingers to her. She rose from the bench and walked away in a dignified manner. But all the evening she thought of him; in imagination seeing the train as it dashed across dark moorlands or through deep, wild ravines near to its destination; seeing the brightly lit compartment, with him in it smoking a cigar or reading a book in the corner by the corridor. He was big and strong, in-clined to be stout even, with smooth red-brown cheeks and a fierce reddish moustache. How old? Forty-five—forty-three at the lowest. With surprising correctness she guessed that he was a com-mercial traveller of some large firm.

On the following Monday he stood as usual at the door of the compartment, and he made a sign to her as if inviting her or order-ing her to approach. She looked up and down the platform to see if her husband or anybody else was observing her, and then went to the carriage.

'What is it?' she asked quietly. 'Do you want a newspaper?'

'No, I wanted to speak to you.'

'Indeed,' said Mrs Read, flushing and using words that she felt were utterly inadequate to so portentous an occasion. 'Then I consider it great cheek your beckoning to me like that. Yes, I do.'

' "He either fears his fate too much!" You're acquainted with the quotation?' and leaning out of the compartment window as if trying to get his face close to hers, he talked in a way that almost took her breath away. He had the glib eloquence that belongs to his profession, and was able to lighten it with the half-facetious tone that will sometimes obtain an order when argument is exhausted. 'O sweet and mysterious lady, who and what are you?

As you are beautiful, be kind. I have named you the Duchess of Tudor Green. That is what you are, isn't it?'

'Certainly not,' she said, still inadequately.

'A countess. A countess at the least.'

'Nothing of the sort.'

'Then what has this dust heap, this back yard of the universe, done to deserve your constant presence?'

She could not help smiling at this, and she told him that she was the wife of the station-master. 'If you must know.'

'But your name.'

'Why should I tell you my name.'

'Because I am going to write to you.'

'No, no.'

'Oh, yes. And I want to address my letter properly. If you don't tell me, I shall address it to The Entrancing Wife of the Tudor Green Station-Master.'

'How can you be so silly? No, indeed.'

She was frightened. She looked at him with an appeal in her eyes and spoke like a child. 'You'd get me into an awful row if you did that.'

'Then give me your name.'

'Take your seats, take your seats,' cried the porters. 'Next stop Leicester.'

'Your name.'

'Read,' she said weakly. 'R-E-A-D.'

Then as the train glided out of the station, she went with slow, heavy footsteps up the stairs to the booking-hall, and up again to the house. Two minutes! It seemed incredible that her husband had dispatched the train within the prescribed time. The train seemed to have been there for hours.

All that evening she was thrilled, excited, but angry with herself. Next morning she woke with a sense of some queer, unexplained sort of happiness, like the memory of a dream; and then, also inexplicably, this gave place to a feeling of even greater blankness and dullness than she had experienced in the past. By ten-thirty she understood and, worse still, mentally acknowledged what was the matter with her. She wanted to see that man again, and the trouble was that between now and the possibility of seeing him, there stretched the appalling stream of empty routine made up by five interminable days. She could not see him till six o'clock on Saturday.

It was mere nonsense his saying he intended to write to her. Of course he would not write.

But he did. The letter was a declaration of love; and she answered it, reproving him. And after this, although they talked to each other so often, they exchanged many letters.

Passengers for the train were more numerous, lots of people got in and out, sometimes the two minutes were all bustle and confusion. Thus everything was favourable to the progress of their flirtation. She told herself thousands of times that it should never be anything more than that. Yet she knew it was very dangerous.

As soon as Mr Read's back was turned she used to go swiftly to the carriage door and stand there, watchful and alert, while their light talk continued. She made it as light as she possibly could.

'What you had better do,' said the man, 'is to come with me one day.'

'Oh, that's likely, isn't it?'

'Why not? Run up north and back next day.'

'Thank you; much obliged,' and she laughed.

Then one day Mr Read saw that she was talking to somebody in the train and asked who it had been.

'So funny,' she said. 'A friend of my cousins—the Lamberts—up at Sheffield.'

'Cousins—Sheffield—Lamberts. I never knew that you had relations up there.'

'Oh, yes—two families. The Lamberts and the Balls. Mother's people, you know.'

He did not know, but he believed her. He had not the faintest suspicion that she was lying.

But thence onward she was more careful. The man, however, had no care; he did reckless, mad things.

'Do look out,' she said anxiously. 'Oh, let me go.'

He had seized her hand and he held it.

'Stop struggling. If you struggle, I'll pull you inside and carry you off with me.' His face was hot and red, and the glib words poured from him. 'Say you love me. I'll make you say it. I'll hold your hand till you say it.'

'Let me go.' She was scared, trying to laugh, almost ready to cry. 'Of course I don't love you. Duchesses don't fall in love with strange men in trains.'

'Be quiet. Nobody's looking. Listen. I shall be off the circuit soon. I shan't come south at all. I'm going to Belgium. Say you like the feel of my hand, really. You want me as much as I want you.'

'I don't. Let me go. Oh, I'll never speak to you again.'

'All right.' He had released her. He stood a little way from the door with his hands plunged in his pockets, and he glared at her. 'You needn't worry. I never want to speak to you again either.' And he seated himself in the furthest corner of the carriage, and sat there with his back towards her. He did not even turn round when the train moved.

That evening she wrote a letter to him, the doubly fatal letter that women always write on such occasions. First, it is fatal to write at all; and, second, it is fatal to say the things they say. But they all seem to do it, employing nearly the same words always. One could write the letter for them.

'It has made me wretchedly miserable,' wrote Mrs Read, 'to know that you are so angry with me. But it is not my fault. You must surely see my point of view. It is all very well for you, but——' And so on and so forth.

Next day she looked as she had described herself, miserable; white, limp, and dejected, as she used to look in the dull, long winter before the train started running. She told old Emma she must do the work unaided. Then, two days later, the post brought her comfort. He was not inexorably angry. She helped Emma, she laughed and sang on the stairs, and from that day she abandoned the famous 'point of view', she thought no more of whether things were right or wrong, wise or foolish, cheap or prodigiously costly. She had determined to tear out of the heart of life all that it can yield before it grows cold and changes to unthrobbing, unfeeling death.

When she told her husband that she would like to go up north, spend a night with her cousins, and come back next day, he made no objection. It seemed to him so natural that she should want to have a trip in the splendid train.

'I suppose,' she said, 'you could get me a free pass, couldn't you?'

'Yes, I suppose so. . . . Oh, no doubt I can,' said Mr Read hopefully; and he added that he would go up to the terminus and ask them at the traffic manager's office this very afternoon.

But they refused to grant the favour. Both mortified and indignant, Mr Read bought a first-class return ticket. He told her that it was a pass, and looked for her delight at seeing that it entitled her to travel first-class. However, she said nothing, until presently, observing that it seemed like an ordinary ticket, she questioned him. Then he was forced to admit that he had bought and paid for it with his own money.

'Oh, but that's too good of you—much too good.' And after a pause she said meditatively, 'Suppose I changed my mind and didn't go, would they give you back your money?'

'I doubt it.'

Why had she asked? She knew that she was going, really.

On the morrow he saw her into the train himself, hurrying her along, seeking a comfortable compartment.

'Here, this will do,' she said, and she turned the handle of a door.

The compartment was empty except for a large man in the far corner. The station-master hesitated. On principle he liked to put ladies with other ladies. But this was a corridor coach. Moreover, Mrs Read had already got in. He handed in the dressing case after her. The big man took no notice of them, not even looking up from his paper.

'Bye-bye,' whispered the station-master; 'take care of yourself.' And he hurried off to his duties.

She did not come back next day. She wrote to say she was never coming back.

Mr Read showed the world a stiff, if rather jerky, sort of dignity in his misfortune and disgrace. Except for a few words with Emma and Inspector Hankinson he refused to speak of the matter, giving out to everybody that his wife would be returning before long. Stupid as was old Emma, she had had suspicions, and in spite of confusion and excitement Hankinson had seen things and thought about them. For one thing he had seen the man in the train. He would know him anywhere.

'You'd know him yourself,' he said. 'You must have spotted him.'

'If you ever see him in the train again, you tell me,' said Mr Read. 'Tell me that instant.'

But the man was never seen again.

One night as Mr Read sat at supper Emma's stupid affection compelled her to touch upon the forbidden subject.

'You don't eat, sir, like you did—and that ain't right with all your work and responsibility. If I may say it, sir, you'd far better stop fretting for her. And b'lieve me, there's as good fish in the sea as ever came out of it.'

The station-master thanked her for her faithful kindliness; but next day he paid her her wages, gave her a present, and dismissed her. He engaged an even older woman, who came for an hour in the morning and in the evening. He pigged it thus as well as he could.

Once, too, Hankinson spoke to him in the gentle, kindly voice of genuine commiseration.

'You know, I am sorry this should have happened.'

'Nothing has happened,' said the station-master, flushing and trembling. 'Mrs Read has gone away for change of air, and will be back soon.'

Throughout the summer he nourished a sort of superstitious belief that his wife would come back to him, but he was unable to prepare or even think of the attitude he should adopt in such an event, although he could see himself and hear himself all day long in imagined scenes when brought face to face with the man. He knew about that all right. He or the man should die.

Nowadays he hated the train. It sickened him and set him trembling as it smoothly crept in; the imagined noise of it when far away filled his brain; the sheer deadly weight of it swung with remorseless force through his dreams. In the torment of his thoughts the train and the man had become all one. Brutal and overwhelming both of them, together they symbolized destiny, destiny that for years ignores you, then comes from afar, knocks you down, passes over you, crushing you like a worm. Sometimes as he stood on an almost empty platform all alone, thinking, he had what the French call an *éblouissement*. Although the signals had not been taken off, although no electric bell had rung, a visionary train was bearing down upon them; it seemed to come tearing and rending space; it flashed past, an invisible whirlwind of iron, steel, woodwork, glass, and steam. Mr Read put a shaky hand to his forehead and shaded his eyes. The whole world was shaking.

He was glad that the train itself had failed to attract. Of course everything in the slightest way connected with him must turn out badly, but in this case he did not mind. He felt pleased. With the beginning of the regular tourist season passengers for the train grew less. Tudor Green people never used it, its coaches became emptier and emptier. By the end of September all the line knew that the allied companies had decided to abandon their experiment. Then soon came the definite announcement that 'as from November first' the train would cease to run.

The station-master watched one of his staff pasting on the bills.

On 30 October the long-distance train passed through on its last northward journey. It was a wretched foggy day, with the fog outside clearing towards evening, but still filling the station, and about seven the station-master, standing on the down platform, had the worst of his *éblouissements*. A miserable, bedraggled woman, getting out of a third-class carriage of a train from London, suddenly emerged upon him like a ghost in shrouds of vapour and touched his arm. It was his wife.

'Step upstairs,' said Mr Read shakily. 'The door's unlocked. I'll follow you soon as I can.... Yes, sir, this is Tudor Green. No, you don't change anywhere for Tide End.'

Her aspect was that of the guilty wife in a melodrama. Her garments were shabby, her face was white, her eyes seemed dark, tragically hollow. As she sat crouching by the fire that the old woman had lighted for her in the living-room and as Mr Read stood looking at her and making vague gestures with his hands, he had a clear vision of her as she used to be not very long ago; so fresh and healthy, when he came to the gate of her mother's house and she was waiting for him in the little garden among the country flowers, a country flower herself, waiting for *him*, her sweetheart. Pity welled up from his tortured heart, flooding him, drowning him. It was his fault, truly. They would say so at the Day of Judgement. She had put herself and her life into his hands, and he had been unable to hold them or protect them. He was a failure.

She confessed that she had been with the man all this while, in Belgium. Now he had cast her off. She wanted her husband to forgive her.

Mr Read said that he would do so.

While she told her tale he was compelled to leave her once or twice and run downstairs to attend to business. When he came back she went on with it again. As soon as she had done she began to cry.

'There, that's enough,' cried Mr Read, gulpingly and huskily. 'We'll make the best of things, not the worst. I've told you I'm prepared to—let bygones—let bygones.... A fresh start together, if—if you'll loyally——' But he could not continue. Suddenly he sat down at the table and wept much more loudly than she. 'Oh, God! All my life! Yet I've tried—never, never have I ceased trying. Oh, my God.'

The old woman came in, laid the table, brought the supper; and later on, when they sat at their meal, they were able to talk quite naturally. In the lamplit peace of the room, with only the noises and tremblings that did not disturb either of them, it was almost like old times. She asked him questions—even a question about the train.

'No, not a success. Coming off. . . . Yes, tomorrow we shall see her last trip.' And he scratched his side whiskers and blinked his eyes.

Then that same night, very late, she made a further confession. She was going to have a child.

This finished him. It was more than he could contend against— this notion of her having a baby and of him not being the father.

Next day the fog had gone. At six o'clock the night was dark and still, with approaching frost in the air. A little interest was displayed when the long-distance train came in for the last time. Ticket collectors descended the steps for the last look; the two barmaids were in the doorway of the refreshment-room; Smith's boys peered into its empty restaurant car. The station-master was there, of course, but he did not so much as glance at it. As the enormous engine loomed up under the footbridge he called to Inspector Hankinson.

'Hankinson, take charge. Hold her the full two minutes. Then shove her off. I'm wanted.'

And he hurried along the platform and disappeared. He had gone down to the path that leads to the southern signal cabin.

Two minutes. The train glided out of the station for the last time. But it stopped again about 400 yards further on and stood there in the darkness, with its tail lamps glowing like luminous blood, people shouting from the signal cabin, the rear guard coming back between the metals, and passengers putting their heads out of windows and asking if there had been an accident.

At the inquest they said it was an accident; and the coroner expressed great sympathy with the widow, who, as he understood, was about to become a mother.

H. G. Wells

Miss Winchelsea's Heart

Miss Winchelsea was going to Rome. The matter had filled her mind for a month or more, and had overflowed so abundantly into her conversation that quite a number of people who were not going to Rome, and who were not likely to go to Rome, had made it a personal grievance against her. Some indeed had attempted quite unavailingly to convince her that Rome was not nearly such a desirable place as it was reported to be, and others had gone so far as to suggest behind her back that she was dreadfully 'stuck up' about 'that Rome of hers'. And little Lily Hardhurst had told her friend Mr Binns that so far as she was concerned Miss Winchelsea might 'go to her old Rome and stop there; *she* (Miss Lily Hardhurst) wouldn't grieve'. And the way in which Miss Winchelsea put herself upon terms of personal tenderness with Horace and Benvenuto Cellini and Raphael and Shelley and Keats—if she had been Shelley's widow she could not have professed a keener interest in his grave—was a matter of universal astonishment. Her dress was a triumph of tactful discretion, sensible but not too 'touristy'— Miss Winchelsea had a great dread of being 'touristy'—and her Baedeker was carried in a cover of grey to hide its glaring red. She made a prim and pleasant little figure on the Charing Cross platform, in spite of her swelling pride, when at last the great day dawned and she could start for Rome. The day was bright, the Channel passage would be pleasant and all the omens promised well. There was the gayest sense of adventure in this unprecedented departure.

She was going with two friends who had been fellow-students with her at the training college, nice honest girls both, though not so good at history and literature as Miss Winchelsea. They both looked up to her immensely, though physically they had to look down, and she anticipated some pleasant times to be spent in 'stirring them up' to her own pitch of æsthetic and historical enthusiasm. They had secured seats already, and welcomed her effusively at the carriage door. In the instant criticism of the encounter she noted that Fanny had a slightly 'touristy' leather strap, and that

Helen had succumbed to a serge jacket with side pockets, into which her hands were thrust. But they were much too happy with themselves and the expedition for their friend to attempt any hint at the moment about these things. As soon as the first ecstasies were over—Fanny's enthusiasm was a little noisy and crude, and consisted mainly in emphatic repetitions of 'Just *fancy*! we're going to Rome, my dear!—Rome!'—they gave their attention to their fellow-travellers. Helen was anxious to secure a compartment to themselves, and, in order to discourage intruders, got out and planted herself firmly on the step. Miss Winchelsea peeped out over her shoulder, and made sly little remarks about the accumulating people on the platform, at which Fanny laughed gleefully.

They were travelling with one of Mr Thomas Gunn's parties—fourteen days in Rome for fourteen pounds. They did not belong to the personally conducted party of course—Miss Winchelsea had seen to that—but they travelled with it because of the convenience of that arrangement. The people were the oddest mixture, and wonderfully amusing. There was a vociferous red-faced polyglot personal conductor in a pepper and salt suit, very long in the arms and legs and very active. He shouted proclamations. When he wanted to speak to people he stretched out an arm and held them until his purpose was accomplished. One hand was full of papers, tickets, counterfoils of tourists. The people of the personally conducted party were, it seemed, of two sorts: people the conductor wanted and could not find, and people he did not want and who followed him in a steadily growing tail up and down the platform. These people seemed, indeed, to think that their one chance of reaching Rome lay in keeping close to him. Three little old ladies were particularly energetic in his pursuit, and at last maddened him to the pitch of clapping them into a carriage and daring them to emerge again. For the rest of the time, one, two, or three of their heads protruded from the window wailing enquiries about 'a little wickerwork box' whenever he drew near. There was a very stout man with a very stout wife in shiny black; there was a little old man like an aged ostler.

'What *can* such people want in Rome?' asked Miss Winchelsea. 'What can it mean to them?' There was a tall curate in a very small straw hat, and a short curate encumbered by a long camera stand. The contrast amused Fanny very much. Once they heard someone calling for 'Snooks'. 'I always thought that name was invented by novelists,' said Miss Winchelsea. 'Fancy! Snooks. I wonder which *is* Mr Snooks.' Finally they picked out a stout and resolute little man in a large check suit. 'If he isn't Snooks, he ought to be,' said Miss Winchelsea.

Presently the conductor discovered Helen's attempt at a corner in carriages. 'Room for five,' he bawled with a parallel translation on his fingers. A party of four together—mother, father, and two daughters—blundered in, all greatly excited. 'It's all right, Ma—you let *me*,' said one of the daughters, hitting her mother's bonnet with a handbag she struggled to put in the rack. Miss Winchelsea detested people who banged about and called their mother 'Ma'. A young man travelling alone followed. He was not at all 'touristy' in his costume, Miss Winchelsea observed; his Gladstone bag was of good pleasant leather with labels reminiscent of Luxembourg and Ostend, and his boots, though brown, were not vulgar. He carried an overcoat on his arm. Before these people had properly settled in their places, came an inspection of tickets and a slamming of doors, and behold! they were gliding out of Charing Cross station on their way to Rome.

'Fancy!' cried Fanny, 'we are going to Rome, my dear! Rome! I don't seem to believe it, even now.'

Miss Winchelsea suppressed Fanny's emotions with a little smile, and the lady who was called 'Ma' explained to people in general why they had 'cut it so close' at the station. The two daughters called her 'Ma' several times, toned her down in a tactless effective way, and drove her at last to the muttered inventory of a basket of travelling requisites. Presently she looked up. 'Lor!' she said, 'I didn't bring *them*!' Both the daughters said 'Oh, Ma!' but what 'them' was did not appear. Presently Fanny produced Hare's *Walks in Rome*, a sort of mitigated guidebook very popular among Roman visitors; and the father of the two daughters began to examine his books of tickets minutely, apparently in a search after English words. When he had looked at the tickets for a long time right way up, he turned them upside down. Then he produced a fountain pen and dated them with considerable care. The young man having completed an unostentatious survey of his fellow travellers produced a book and fell to reading. When Helen and Fanny were looking out of the window at Chislehurst—the place interested Fanny because the poor dear Empress of the French used to live there—Miss Winchelsea took the opportunity to observe the book the young man held. It was not a guidebook but a thin volume of poetry—*bound*. She glanced at his face—it seemed a refined pleasant face to her hasty glance. He wore a gilt *pince-nez*.

'Do you think she lives there now?' said Fanny, and Miss Winchelsea's inspection came to an end.

For the rest of the journey Miss Winchelsea talked little, and what she said was as pleasant and as stamped with refinement as she could make it. Her voice was always low and clear and pleasant, and she took care that on this occasion it was particularly low and clear and pleasant. As they came under the white cliffs the young man put his book of poetry away, and when at last the train stopped beside the boat, he displayed a graceful alacrity with the impedimenta of Miss Winchelsea and her friends. Miss Winchelsea 'hated nonsense', but she was pleased to see the young man perceived at once that they were ladies, and helped them without any violent geniality; and how nicely he showed that his civilities were to be no excuse for further intrusions. None of her party had been out of England before, and they were all excited and nervous at the Channel passage. They stood in a little group in a good place near the middle of the boat—the young man had taken Miss Winchelsea's hold-all there and had told her it was a good place—and they watched the white shores of Albion recede and quoted Shakespeare and made quiet fun of their fellow travellers in the English way.

They were particularly amused at the precautions the bigger-sized people had taken against the waves—cut lemons and flasks prevailed, one lady lay full length in a deck chair with a handkerchief over her face, and a very broad resolute man in a bright brown 'touristy' suit walked all the way from England to France along the deck, with his legs as widely apart as Providence permitted. These were all excellent precautions, and nobody was ill. The personally conducted party pursued the conductor about the deck with enquiries, in a manner that suggested to Helen's mind the rather vulgar image of hens with a piece of bacon peel, until at last he went into hiding below. And the young man with the thin volume of poetry stood in the stern watching England receding, looking, to Miss Winchelsea's eye, rather lonely and sad.

And then came Calais and tumultuous novelties, and the young man had not forgotten Miss Winchelsea's hold-all and the other little things. All three girls, though they had passed government examinations in French to any extent, were stricken with a dumb shame of their accents, and the young man was very useful. And he did not intrude. He put them in a comfortable carriage and raised his hat and went away. Miss Winchelsea thanked him in her best manner—a pleasing cultivated manner—and Fanny said he was 'nice' almost before he was out of earshot. 'I wonder what he can be,' said Helen. 'He's going to Italy, because I noticed green tickets in his book.' Miss Winchelsea almost told them of the poetry, and decided not to do so. And presently the carriage windows seized hold upon them and the young man was forgotten. It made them feel that they were doing an educated sort of thing to travel through a country whose commonest advertisements were in idiomatic French, and Miss Winchelsea made unpatriotic comparisons because there were weedy little sign-board advertisements by the rail side instead of the broad hoardings that deface the landscape in our land. But the north of France is really uninteresting country, and after a time Fanny reverted to Hare's *Walks* and Helen initiated lunch. Miss Winchelsea awoke out of a happy reverie; she had been trying to realize, she said, that she was actually going to Rome, but she perceived at Helen's suggestion that she was hungry, and they lunched out of their baskets very cheerfully. In the afternoon they were tired and silent until Helen made tea. Miss Winchelsea might have dozed, only she knew Fanny slept with her mouth open; and as their fellow passengers were two rather nice critical-looking ladies of uncertain age—who knew French well enough to talk it—she employed herself in keeping Fanny awake. The rhythm of the train became insistent, and the streaming landscape outside at last quite painful to the eye. Before their night's stoppage came they were already dreadfully tired of travelling.

The stoppage for the night was brightened by the appearance of the young man, and his manners were all that could be desired and his French quite serviceable. His coupons availed for the same hotel as theirs, and by chance as it seemed he sat next to Miss Winchelsea at the *table d'hôte*. In spite of her enthusiasm for Rome, she had thought out some such possibility very thoroughly, and when he ventured to make a remark upon the tediousness of travelling— he let the soup and fish go by before he did this—she did not simply assent to his proposition, but responded with another. They were soon comparing their journeys, and Helen and Fanny were cruelly overlooked in the conversation. It was to be the same journey, they found; one day for the galleries at Florence—'from what I hear,' said the young man, 'it is barely enough'—and the rest at Rome. He talked of Rome very pleasantly; he was evidently quite well read, and he quoted Horace about Soracte. Miss Winchelsea had 'done' that book of Horace for her matriculation, and was delighted to cap his quotation. It gave a sort of tone to things, this incident—a touch of refinement to mere chatting. Fanny expressed a few emotions, and Helen interpolated a few sensible remarks, but the bulk of the talk on the girls' side naturally fell to Miss Winchelsea.

Before they reached Rome this young man was tacitly of their party. They did not know his name nor what he was, but it seemed he taught, and Miss Winchelsea had a shrewd idea he was an extension lecturer. At any rate he was something of that sort, something gentlemanly and refined without being opulent and impossible. She tried once or twice to ascertain whether he came from Oxford or Cambridge, but he missed her timid opportunities. She tried to get him to make remarks about those places to see if he would say 'go up' to them instead of 'go down'—she knew that was how you told a 'Varsity man. He used the word ''Varsity'—not university—in quite the proper way.

They saw as much of Mr Ruskin's Florence as their brief time permitted; the young man met them in the Pitti Gallery and went round with them, chatting brightly, and evidently very grateful for their recognition. He knew a great deal about art, and all four enjoyed the morning immensely. It was fine to go round recognizing old favourites and finding new beauties, especially while so many people fumbled helplessly with Baedeker. Nor was he a bit of a prig, Miss Winchelsea said, and indeed she detested prigs. He had a distinct undertow of humour, and was funny, for example, without being vulgar, at the expense of the quaint work of Beato Angelico. He had a grave seriousness beneath it all, and was quick to seize the moral lessons of the pictures. Fanny went softly among these masterpieces; she admitted 'she knew so little about them', and she confessed that to her they were 'all beautiful'. Fanny's 'beautiful' inclined to be a little monotonous, Miss Winchelsea thought. She had been quite glad when the last sunny Alp had vanished, because of the staccato of Fanny's admiration. Helen said little, but Miss Winchelsea had found her a little wanting on the æsthetic side in the old days and was not surprised; sometimes she laughed at the young man's hesitating delicate little jests and sometimes she didn't, and sometimes she seemed quite lost to the art about them in the contemplation of the dresses of the other visitors.

At Rome the young man was with them intermittently. A rather 'touristy' friend of his took him away at times. He complained comically to Miss Winchelsea. 'I have only two short weeks in Rome,' he said, 'and my friend Leonard wants to spend a whole day at Tivoli looking at a waterfall.'

'What is your friend Leonard?' asked Miss Winchelsea abruptly.

'He's the most enthusiastic pedestrian I ever met,' the young man replied—amusingly, but a little unsatisfactorily, Miss Winchelsea thought.

They had some glorious times, and Fanny could not think what they would have done without him. Miss Winchelsea's interest and Fanny's enormous capacity for admiration were insatiable. They never flagged—through pictures and sculpture galleries, immense crowded churches, ruins and museums, Judas trees and prickly pears, wine carts and palaces, they admired their way unflinchingly. They never saw a stone pine nor a eucalyptus but they named and admired it; they never glimpsed Soracte but they exclaimed. Their common ways were made wonderful by imaginative play. 'Here Cæsar may have walked,' they would say. 'Raphael may have seen Soracte from this very point.' They happened on the tomb of Bibulus. 'Old Bibulus,' said the young man. 'The oldest monument of Republican Rome!' said Miss Winchelsea.

'I'm dreadfully stupid,' said Fanny, 'but who *was* Bibulus?'

There was a curious little pause.

'Wasn't he the person who built the wall?' said Helen.

The young man glanced quickly at her and laughed. 'That was Balbus,' he said. Helen reddened, but neither he nor Miss Winchelsea threw any light upon Fanny's ignorance about Bibulus.

Helen was more taciturn than the other three, but then she was always taciturn; and usually she took care of the tram tickets and things like that, or kept her eye on them if the young man took them, and told him where they were when he wanted them. Glorious times they had, these young people, in that pale brown cleanly city of memories that was once the world. Their only sorrow was the shortness of the time. They said indeed that the electric trams and the '70 buildings, and that criminal advertisement that glares upon the Forum, outraged their æsthetic feelings unspeakably; but that was only part of the fun. And indeed Rome is such a wonderful place that at times it made Miss Winchelsea forget some of her most carefully prepared enthusiasms, and Helen, taken unawares, would suddenly admit the beauty of unexpected things. Yet Fanny and Helen would have liked a shop window or so in the English quarter if Miss Winchelsea's uncompromising hostility to all other English visitors had not rendered that district impossible.

The intellectual and æsthetic fellowship of Miss Winchelsea and the scholarly young man passed insensibly towards a deeper feeling. The exuberant Fanny did her best to keep pace with their recondite admiration by playing her 'beautiful' with vigour, and saying 'Oh! *let's* go', with enormous appetite whenever a new place of interest was mentioned. But Helen towards the end developed a certain want of sympathy, that disappointed Miss Winchelsea a little. She refused to 'see anything' in the face of Beatrice Cenci— Shelley's Beatrice Cenci!—in the Barberini gallery; and one day, when they were deploring the electric trams, she said rather snappishly that 'people must get about somehow, and it's better than torturing horses up these horrid little hills'. She spoke of the Seven Hills of Rome as 'horrid little hills'!

And the day they went on the Palatine—though Miss Winchelsea did not know of this—she remarked suddenly to Fanny, 'Don't hurry like that, my dear; *they* don't want us to overtake them. And we don't say the right things for them when we *do* get near.'

'I wasn't trying to overtake them,' said Fanny, slackening her excessive pace; 'I wasn't indeed.' And for a minute she was short of breath.

But Miss Winchelsea had come upon happiness. It was only when she came to look back across an intervening tragedy that she quite realized how happy she had been, pacing among the cypress-shadowed ruins, and exchanging the very highest class of information the human mind can possess, the most refined impressions it is possible to convey. Insensibly emotion crept into their intercourse, sunning itself openly and pleasantly at last when Helen's modernity was not too near. Insensibly their interest drifted from the wonderful associations about them to their more intimate and personal feelings. In a tentative way information was supplied; she spoke allusively of her school, of her examination successes, of her gladness that the days of 'Cram' were over. He made it quite clear that he also was a teacher. They spoke of the greatness of their calling, of the necessity of sympathy to face its irksome details, of a certain loneliness they sometimes felt.

That was in the Colosseum, and it was as far as they got that day, because Helen returned with Fanny—she had taken her into the upper galleries. Yet the private dreams of Miss Winchelsea, already vivid and concrete enough, became now realistic in the highest degree. She figured that pleasant young man, lecturing in the most edifying way to his students, herself modestly prominent as his intellectual mate and helper; she figured a refined little home, with two bureaux, with white shelves of high-class books, and autotypes of the pictures of Rossetti and Burne-Jones, with Morris's wall papers and flowers in pots of beaten copper. Indeed she figured many things. On the Pincio the two had a few precious moments together, while Helen marched Fanny off to see the *muro Torto*, and he spoke at once plainly. He said he hoped their friendship was only beginning, that he already found her company very precious to him, that indeed it was more than that.

He became nervous, thrusting at his glasses with trembling fingers as though he fancied his emotions made them unstable. 'I should of course,' he said, 'tell you things about myself. I know it is rather unusual my speaking to you like this. Only our meeting has been so accidental—or providential—and I am snatching at things. I came to Rome expecting a lonely tour ... and I have been so very happy, so very happy. Quite recently I have found myself in a position—I have dared to think—— And——'

He glanced over his shoulder and stopped. He said 'Demn!' quite distinctly—and she did not condemn him for that manly lapse into profanity. She looked and saw his friend Leonard advancing. He drew nearer; he raised his hat to Miss Winchelsea, and his smile was almost a grin. 'I've been looking for you everywhere, Snooks,' he said. 'You promised to be on the Piazza steps half an hour ago.'

Snooks! The name struck Miss Winchelsea like a blow in the face. She did not hear his reply. She thought afterwards that Leonard must have considered her the vaguest-minded person. To this day she is not sure whether she was introduced to Leonard or not, nor what she said to him. A sort of mental paralysis was upon her. Of all offensive surnames—Snooks!

Helen and Fanny were returning, there were civilities, and the young men were receding. By a great effort she controlled herself to face the enquiring eyes of her friends. All that afternoon she lived the life of a heroine under the indescribable outrage of that name, chatting, observing, with 'Snooks' gnawing at her heart. From the moment that it first rang upon her ears, the dream of her happiness was prostrate in the dust. All the refinement she had figured was ruined and defaced by that cognomen's inexorable vulgarity.

What was that refined little home to her now, in spite of autotypes, Morris papers, and bureaux? Athwart it in letters of fire ran an incredible inscription: 'Mrs Snooks'. That may seem a small thing to the reader, but consider the delicate refinement of Miss Winchelsea's mind. Be as refined as you can and then think of writing yourself down: 'Snooks'. She conceived herself being addressed as Mrs Snooks by all the people she liked least, conceived the patronymic touched with a vague quality of insult. She figured a card of grey and silver bearing 'Winchelsea' triumphantly effaced by an arrow, Cupid's arrow, in favour of 'Snooks'. Degrading confession of feminine weakness! She imagined the terrible rejoicings of certain girl friends, of certain grocer cousins from whom her growing refinement had long since estranged her. How they would make it sprawl across the envelope that would bring their sarcastic congratulations. Would even his pleasant company compensate her for that? 'It is impossible,' she muttered; 'impossible! *Snooks!*'

She was sorry for him, but not so sorry as she was for herself. For him she had a touch of indignation. To be so nice, so refined, while all the time he was 'Snooks', to hide under a pretentious gentility of demeanour the badge sinister of his surname seemed a sort of treachery. To put it in the language of sentimental science she felt he had 'led her on'.

There were of course moments of terrible vacillation, a period even when something almost like passion bid her throw refinement to the winds. And there was something in her, an unexpurgated vestige of vulgarity that made a strenuous attempt at proving that Snooks was not so very bad a name after all. Any hovering hesitation flew before Fanny's manner, when Fanny came with an air of catastrophe to tell that she also knew the horror. Fanny's voice fell to a whisper when she said *Snooks*. Miss Winchelsea would not give him any answer when at last, in the Borghese, she could have a minute with him; but she promised him a note.

She handed him that note in the little book of poetry he had lent her, the little book that had first drawn them together. Her refusal was ambiguous, allusive. She could no more tell him why she rejected him than she could have told a cripple of his hump. He too must feel something of the unspeakable quality of his name. Indeed he had avoided a dozen chances of telling it, she now perceived. So she spoke of 'obstacles she could not reveal'—'reasons why the thing he spoke of was impossible'. She addressed the note with a shiver, 'E. K. Snooks.'

Things were worse than she had dreaded; he asked her to explain. How *could* she explain? Those last two days in Rome were dreadful. She was haunted by his air of astonished perplexity. She knew she had given him intimate hopes, she had not the courage to examine her mind thoroughly for the extent of her encouragement. She knew he must think her the most changeable of beings. Now that she was in full retreat, she would not even perceive his hints of a possible correspondence. But in that matter he did a thing that seemed to her at once delicate and romantic. He made a go-between of Fanny. Fanny could not keep the secret, and came and told her that night under a transparent pretext of needed advice. 'Mr Snooks,' said Fanny, 'wants to write to me. Fancy! I had no idea. But should I let him?' They talked it over long and earnestly, and Miss Winchelsea was careful to keep the veil over her heart. She was already repenting his disregarded hints. Why should she not hear of him sometimes—painful though his name must be to her? Miss Winchelsea decided it might be permitted, and Fanny kissed her good-night with unusual emotion. After she had gone Miss Winchelsea sat for a long time at the window of her little room. It was moonlight, and down the street a man sang 'Santa Lucia' with almost heart-dissolving tenderness.... She sat very still.

She breathed a word very softly to herself. The word was *'Snooks'*. Then she got up with a profound sigh, and went to bed. The next morning he said to her meaningly, 'I shall hear of you through your friend.'

Mr Snooks saw them off from Rome with that pathetic interrogative perplexity still on his face, and if it had not been for Helen he would have retained Miss Winchelsea's hold-all in his hand as a sort of encyclopædic keepsake. On their way back to England Miss Winchelsea on six separate occasions made Fanny promise to write to her the longest of long letters. Fanny, it seemed, would be quite near Mr Snooks. Her new school—she was always going to new schools—would be only five miles from Steely Bank, and it was in the Steely Bank Polytechnic, and one or two first-class schools, that Mr Snooks did his teaching. He might even see her at times. They could not talk much of him—she and Fanny always spoke of 'him', never of Mr Snooks—because Helen was apt to say unsympathetic things about him. Her nature had coarsened very much, Miss Winchelsea perceived, since the old Training College days; she had become hard and cynical. She thought he had a weak face, mistaking refinement for weakness as people of her stamp are apt to do, and when she heard his name was Snooks, she said she had expected something of the sort. Miss Winchelsea was careful to spare her own feelings after that, but Fanny was less circumspect.

The girls parted in London, and Miss Winchelsea returned, with a new interest in life, to the Girls' High School in which she had been an increasingly valuable assistant for the last three years. Her new interest in life was Fanny as a correspondent, and to give her a lead she wrote her a lengthy descriptive letter within a fortnight of her return. Fanny answered very disappointingly. Fanny indeed had no literary gift, but it was new to Miss Winchelsea to find herself deploring the want of gifts in a friend. That letter was even criticized aloud in the safe solitude of Miss Winchelsea's study, and her criticism, spoken with great bitterness, was 'Twaddle!' It was full of just the things Miss Winchelsea's letter had been full of, particulars of the school. And of Mr Snooks, only this much: 'I have had a letter from Mr Snooks, and he has been over to see me on two Saturday afternoons running. He talked about Rome and you; we both talked about you. Your ears must have burnt, my dear. . . .'

Miss Winchelsea repressed a desire to demand more explicit information, and wrote the sweetest long letter again. 'Tell me all about yourself, dear. That journey has quite refreshed our ancient friendship, and I do so want to keep in touch with you.' About Mr Snooks she simply wrote on the fifth page that she was glad Fanny had seen him, and that if he *should* ask after her, she was to be remembered to him *very kindly* (underlined). And Fanny replied most obtusely in the key of that 'ancient friendship', reminding Miss Winchelsea of a dozen foolish things of those old schoolgirl days at the training college, and saying not a word about Mr Snooks!

For nearly a week Miss Winchelsea was so angry at the failure of Fanny as a go-between that she could not write to her. And then she wrote less effusively, and in her letter she asked point blank, 'Have you seen Mr Snooks?' Fanny's letter was unexpectedly satisfactory. 'I *have* seen Mr Snooks,' she wrote, and having once named him she kept on about him; it was all Snooks—Snooks this and Snooks that. He was to give a public lecture, said Fanny, among other things. Yet Miss Winchelsea, after the first glow of gratification, still found this letter a little unsatisfactory. Fanny did not report Mr Snooks as saying anything about Miss Winchelsea, nor as looking white and worn, as he ought to have been doing. And behold! before she had replied, came a second letter from Fanny on the same theme, quite a gushing letter, and covering six sheets with her loose feminine hand.

And about this second letter was a rather odd little thing that Miss Winchelsea only noticed as she re-read it the third time. Fanny's natural femininity had prevailed even against the round and clear traditions of the training college; she was one of those she-creatures born to make all her *m*'s and *n*'s and *u*'s and *r*'s and *e*'s alike, and to leave her *o*'s and *a*'s open and her *i*'s undotted. So that it was only after an elaborate comparison of word with word that Miss Winchelsea felt assured Mr Snooks was not really 'Mr Snooks' at all! In Fanny's first letter of gush he was Mr 'Snooks', in her second the spelling was changed to Mr 'Senoks'. Miss Winchelsea's hand positively trembled as she turned the sheet over—it meant so much to her. For it had already begun to seem to her that even the name of Mrs Snooks might be avoided at too great a price, and suddenly—this possibility! She turned over the six sheets, all dappled with that critical name, and everywhere the first letter had the form of an *e*! For a time she walked the room with a hand pressed upon her heart.

She spent a whole day pondering this change, weighing a letter of enquiry that should be at once discreet and effectual, weighing too what action she should take after the answer came. She was resolved that if this altered spelling was anything more than a quaint fancy of Fanny's, she would write forthwith to Mr Snooks. She had now reached a stage when the minor refinements of behaviour disappear. Her excuse remained uninvented but she had the subject of her letter clear in her mind, even to the hint that 'circumstances in my life have changed very greatly since we talked together'. But she never gave that hint. There came a third letter from that fitful correspondent Fanny. The first line proclaimed her 'the happiest girl alive'.

Miss Winchelsea crushed the letter in her hand—the rest unread—and sat with her face suddenly very still. She had received it just before morning school, and had opened it when the junior mathematicians were well under way. Presently she resumed reading with an appearance of great calm. But after the first sheet she went on reading the third without discovering the error: 'told him frankly I did not like his name,' the third sheet began. 'He told me he did not like it himself—you know that sort of sudden frank way he has'—Miss Winchelsea did know. 'So I said, "Couldn't you change it?" He didn't see it at first. Well, you know, dear, he had told me what it really meant; it means Sevenoaks, only it has got down to Snooks—both Snooks and Noaks, dreadfully vulgar surnames though they be, are really worn forms of Sevenoaks. So I said—even I have my bright ideas at times—"if it got down from Sevenoaks to Snooks, why not get it back from Snooks to Sevenoaks?" And the long and the short of it is, dear, he couldn't refuse me, and he changed his spelling there and then to Senoks for the bills of the new lecture. And afterwards, when we are married, we shall put in the apostrophe and make it Se'noks. Wasn't it kind of him to mind that fancy of mine, when many men would have taken offence? But it is just like him all over; he is as kind as he is clever. Because he knew as well as I did that I would have had him in spite of it, had he been ten times Snooks. But he did it all the same.'

The class was startled by the sound of paper being viciously torn, and looked up to see Miss Winchelsea white in the face, and with some very small pieces of paper clenched in one hand. For a few seconds they stared at her stare, and then her expression changed back to a more familiar one. 'Has anyone finished number three?' she asked in an even tone. She remained calm after that. But impositions ruled high that day. And she spent two laborious evenings writing letters of various sorts to Fanny, before she found a decent congratulatory vein. Her reason struggled hopelessly against the persuasion that Fanny had behaved in an exceedingly treacherous manner.

One may be extremely refined and still capable of a very sore heart. Certainly Miss Winchelsea's heart was very sore. She had moods of sexual hostility, in which she generalized uncharitably about mankind. 'He forgot himself with me,' she said. 'But Fanny is pink and pretty and soft and a fool—a very excellent match for a Man.' And by way of a wedding present she sent Fanny a gracefully bound volume of poetry by George Meredith, and Fanny wrote back a grossly happy letter to say that it was '*all* beautiful'. Miss Winchelsea hoped that some day Mr Senoks might take up that slim book and think for a moment of the donor. Fanny wrote several times before and about her marriage, pursuing that fond legend of their 'ancient friendship', and giving her happiness in the fullest detail. And Miss Winchelsea wrote to Helen for the first time after the Roman journey, saying nothing about the marriage, but expressing very cordial feelings.

They had been in Rome at Easter, and Fanny was married in the August vacation. She wrote a garrulous letter to Miss Winchelsea, describing her home-coming, and the astonishing arrangements of their 'teeny weeny' little house. Mr Se'noks was now beginning to assume a refinement in Miss Winchelsea's memory out of all proportion to the facts of the case, and she tried in vain to imagine his cultured greatness in a 'teeny weeny' little house. 'Am busy enamelling a cosy corner,' said Fanny, sprawling to the end of her third sheet, 'so excuse more.' Miss Winchelsea answered in her best style, gently poking fun at Fanny's arrangements, and hoping intensely that Mr Se'noks might see the letter. Only this hope enabled her to write at all, answering not only that letter but one in November and one at Christmas.

The two latter communications contained urgent invitations for her to come to Steely Bank on a visit during the Christmas holidays. She tried to think that *he* had told her to ask that, but it was too much like Fanny's opulent good nature. She could not but believe that he must be sick of his blunder by this time; and she had more than a hope that he would presently write her a letter beginning 'Dear Friend'. Something subtly tragic in the separation was a great support to her, a sad misunderstanding. To have been jilted would have been intolerable. But he never wrote that letter beginning 'Dear Friend'.

For two years Miss Winchelsea could not go to Steely Bank, in spite of the reiterated invitations of Mrs Sevenoaks—it became full Sevenoaks in the second year. Then one day near the Easter rest she felt lonely and without a soul to understand her in the world, and her mind ran once more on what is called Platonic friendship. Fanny was clearly happy and busy in her new sphere of domesticity, but no doubt *he* had his lonely hours. Did he ever think of those days in Rome—gone now beyond recalling? No one had understood her as he had done; no one in all the world. It would be a sort of melancholy pleasure to talk to him again, and what harm could it do? Why should she deny herself? That night she wrote a sonnet, all but the last two lines of the octave—which would not come, and the next day she composed a graceful little note to tell Fanny she was coming down.

And so she saw him again.

Even at the first encounter it was evident he had changed; he seemed stouter and less nervous, and it speedily appeared that his conversation had already lost much of its old delicacy. There even seemed a justification for Helen's discovery of weakness in his face—in certain lights it *was* weak. He seemed busy and preoccupied about his affairs, and almost under the impression that Miss Winchelsea had come for the sake of Fanny. He discussed his dinner with Fanny in an intelligent way. They only had one good long talk together, and that came to nothing. He did not refer to Rome, and spent some time abusing a man who had stolen an idea he had had for a text book. It did not seem a very wonderful idea to Miss Winchelsea. She discovered he had forgotten the names of more than half the painters whose work they had rejoiced over in Florence.

It was a sadly disappointing week, and Miss Winchelsea was glad when it came to an end. Under various excuses she avoided visiting them again. After a time the visitor's room was occupied by two little boys, and Fanny's invitations ceased. The intimacy of her letters had long since faded away.

Enemies

When Mrs Clara Hansen travels, she keeps herself to herself. This is usually easy, for she has money, has been a baroness and a beauty, and has survived dramatic suffering. The crushing presence of these states in her face and bearing is nearly always enough to stop the loose mouths of people who find themselves in her company. It is only the very stupid, the senile, or the self-obsessed who blunder up to assail that face, withdrawn as a castle, across the common ground of a public dining room.

Last month, when Mrs Hansen left Cape Town for Johannesburg by train, an old lady occupying the adjoining compartment tried to make of her apologies, as she pressed past in the corridor loaded with string bags and paper parcels, an excuse to open one of those pointless conversations between strangers which arise in the nervous moments of departure. Mrs Hansen was giving last calm instructions to Alfred, her Malay chauffeur and manservant, whom she was leaving behind, and she did not look up. Alfred had stowed her old calf cases from Europe firmly and within reach in her compartment, which, of course, influence with the reservation office had ensured she would have to herself all the way. He had watched her put away in a special pocket in her handbag, her train ticket, a ticket for her de luxe bed, a book of tickets for her meals. He had made sure that she had her two yellow sleeping pills and the red pills for that feeling of pressure in her head, lying in cottonwool in her silver pillbox. He himself had seen that her two pairs of spectacles, one for distance, one for reading, were in her overnight bag, and had noted that her lorgnette hung below the diamond bow on the bosom of her dress. He had taken down the folding table from its niche above the washbasin in the compartment, and placed on it the three magazines she had sent him to buy at the bookstall, along with the paper from Switzerland that, this week, had been kept aside, unread, for the journey.

For a full fifteen minutes before the train left, he and his employer were free to ignore the to-and-fro of voices and luggage, the heat and confusion. Mrs Hansen murmured down to him;

Alfred, chauffeur's cap in hand, dusty sunlight the colour of beer dimming the oil shine of his black hair, looked up from the platform and made low assent. They used the half-sentences, the hesitations, and the slight changes of tone or expression of people who speak the language of their association in the country of their own range of situation. It was hardly speech; now and then it sank away altogether into the minds of each, but the sounds of the station did not well up in its place. Alfred dangled the key of the car on his little finger. The old face beneath the toque noted it, and the lips, the infinitely weary corners of the eyes drooped in the indication of a smile. Would he really put the car away into the garage for six weeks after he'd seen that it was oiled and greased?

Unmindful of the finger, his face empty of the satisfaction of a month's wages in advance in his pocket, two friends waiting to be picked up in a house in the Malay quarter of the town, he said, 'I must make a note that I mustn't send Madam's letters on after the twenty-sixth.'

'No. Not later than the twenty-sixth.'

Did she know? With that face that looked as if it knew everything, could she know, too, about the two friends in the house in the Malay quarter?

She said—and neither of them listened—'In case of need, you've always got Mr Van Dam.' Van Dam was her lawyer. This remark, like a stone thrown idly into a pool to pass the time, had fallen time and again between them into the widening hiatus of parting. They had never questioned or troubled to define its meaning. In ten years, what need had there ever been that Alfred couldn't deal with himself, from a burst pipe in the flat to a jammed fastener on Mrs Hansen's dress?

Alfred backed away from the ice-cream carton a vender thrust under his nose; the last untidy lump of canvas luggage belonging to the woman next door thumped down like a dusty animal at Mrs Hansen's side; the final bell rang.

As the train ground past out of the station, Alfred stood quite still with his cap between his hands, watching Mrs Hansen. He always stood like that when he saw her off. And she remained at the window, as usual, smiling slightly, inclining her head slightly, as if in dismissal. Neither waved. Neither moved until the other was borne out of sight.

When the station was gone and Mrs Hansen turned slowly to enter her compartment to the quickening rhythm of the train, she met the gasping face of the old woman next door. Fat overflowed not only from her jowl to her neck, but from her ankles to her shoes. She looked like a pudding that had risen too high and run down the sides of the dish. She was sprinkling cologne on to a handkerchief and hitting with it at her face as if she were trying to kill something. 'Rush like that, it's no good for you,' she said. 'Something went wrong with my son-in-law's car, and what a job to get a taxi! *They* don't care—get you here today or tomorrow. I thought I'd never get up those steps.'

Mrs Hansen looked at her. 'When one is no longer young, one must always give oneself exactly twice as much time as one needs. I have learned that. I beg your pardon.' And she passed before the woman into her compartment.

The woman stopped her in the doorway. 'I wonder if they're serving tea yet? Shall we go along to the dining car?'

'I always have my tea brought to me in my compartment,' said Mrs Hansen, in the low, dead voice that had been considered a pity in her day but that now made young people who could have been her grandchildren ask if she had been an actress. And she slid the door shut.

Alone, she stood a moment in the secretive privacy, where everything swayed and veered in obedience to the gait of the train. She began to look anxiously over the stacked luggage, her lips moving, but she had grown too set to adjust her balance from moment to moment, and suddenly she found herself sitting down. The train had dumped her out of the way. Good thing, too, she thought, chastizing herself impatiently—counting the luggage, fussing, when in ten years Alfred's never forgotten anything. Old fool, she told herself, old fool. Her ageing self often seemed to her an enemy of her real self, the self that had never changed. The enemy was a stupid one, fortunately; she merely had to keep an eye on it in order to keep it outwitted. Other selves that had arisen in her life had been much worse; how terrible had been the struggle with some of *them*!

She sat down with her back to the engine, beside the window, and put on her reading glasses and took up the newspaper from Switzerland. But for some minutes she did not read. She heard again inside herself the words *alone, alone*, just the way she had heard them fifty-nine years ago when she was twelve years old and crossing France by herself for the first time. As she had sat there, bolt upright in the corner of a carriage, her green velvet fur-trimmed cloak around her, her hamper beside her, and the locket with the picture of her grandfather hidden in her hand, she had felt a swelling terror of exhilaration, the dark, drowning swirl of cutting loose, had tasted the strength to be brewed out of self-pity and the calm to be lashed together out of panic that belonged to other times and other journeys approaching her from the distance of her future. *Alone, alone.* This that her real self had known years before it happened to her—before she had lived the journey that took her from a lover, or those others that took her from the alienated faces of madness and death—that same self remembered years after those journeys had dropped behind into the past. Now she was alone, lonely, lone—whatever you liked to call it—all the time. There is nothing of the drama of an occasion about it, for me, she reminded herself dryly. Still, there was no denying it, *alone* was not the same as *lonely*; even the Old Fool could not blur the distinction of that. The blue silk coat quivered where Alfred had hung it, the bundle of magazines edged along the table, and somewhere above her head a loose strap tapped. She felt again aloneness as the carapace that did not shut her off but shielded her strong sense of survival—against it, and all else.

She opened the paper from Switzerland, and, with her left foot (the heat had made it a little swollen) up on the seat opposite, she began to read. She felt lulled and comfortable and was not even irritated by the thuds and dragging noises coming from the partition behind her head; it was clear that that was the woman next door—*she* must be fussing with her luggage. Presently a steward brought a tea tray, which Alfred had ordered before the train left. Mrs Hansen drew in her mouth with pleasure at the taste of the strong tea, as connoisseurs do when they drink old brandy, and read the afternoon away.

She took her dinner in the dining car because she had established in a long experience that it was not a meal that could be expected to travel train corridors and remain hot, and also because there was something shabby, something *petit bourgeois*, about taking meals in the stuffy cubicle in which you were also to sleep. She tidied her hair around the sides of her toque—it was a beautiful hat, one of four, always the same shape, that she had made for herself every second year in Vienna—took off her rings and washed her hands, and powdered her nose, pulling a critical, amused face at herself in the compact mirror. Then she put on her silk coat, picked up her handbag, and went with upright dignity, despite the twitchings and lurchings of the train, along the corridors to the dining car. She seated herself at an empty table for two beside a window, and, of course, although it was early and there were many other seats vacant, the old woman from the compartment next door, entering five minutes later, came straight over and sat down opposite her.

Now it was impossible not to speak to the woman and Mrs Hansen listened to her with the distant patience of an adult giving half an ear to a child, and answered her when necessary, with a dry simplicity calculated to be far above her head. Of course, Old Fool was tempted to unbend, to lapse into the small boastings and rivalries usual between two old ladies. But Mrs Hansen would not allow it and certainly not with this woman—this acquaintance thrust upon her in a train. It was bad enough that, only the week before, Old Fool had led her into one of these pathetic pieces of senile nonsense, cleverly disguised—Old Fool could be wily enough—but, just the same, unmistakably the kind of thing that people found boring. It was about her teeth. At seventy-one they were still her own, which was a self-evident miracle. Yet she had allowed herself, at a dinner party given by some young friends who were obviously impressed by her, to tell a funny story (not quite true, either) about how, when she was a weekend guest in a house with an over-solicitous hostess, the jovial host had hoaxed his wife by impressing upon her the importance of providing a suitable receptacle for their guest's teeth when she took them out overnight. There was a glass beside the jug of water on the bedside table; the hostess appeared, embarrassedly, with another. 'But, my dear, what is the other glass for?' The denouement, laughter, etc. Disgusting. Good teeth as well as bad aches and pains must be kept to oneself; when one is young, one takes the first for granted, and does not know the existence of the others.

So it was that when the menu was held before the two women Mrs Hansen ignored the consternation into which it seemed to plunge her companion, forestalled the temptation to enter, by contributing her doctor's views, into age's passionate preoccupation with diet, and ordered fish.

'D'you think the fish'll be all right? I always wonder, on a train, you know ...,' said the woman from the next compartment.

Mrs Hansen merely confirmed her order to the waiter by lowering her eyes and settling her chin slightly. The woman decided to begin at the beginning, with soup. 'Can't go far wrong with soup, can you?'

'Don't wait, please,' said Mrs Hansen when the soup came.

The soup was watery, the woman said. Mrs Hansen smiled her tragic smile, indulgently. The woman decided that she'd keep Mrs

Hansen company, and risk the fish, too. The fish lay beneath a pasty blanket of white sauce and while Mrs Hansen calmly pushed aside the sauce and ate, the woman said, 'There's nothing like the good, clean food cooked in your own kitchen.'

Mrs Hansen put a forkful of fish to her mouth and, when she had finished it, spoke at last. 'I'm afraid it's many years since I had my own kitchen for more than a month or two a year.'

'Well, of course, if you go about a lot, you get used to strange food, I suppose. I find I can't eat half the stuff they put in front of you in hotels. Last time I was away, there were some days I didn't know what to have at all for lunch. I was in one of the best hotels in Durban and all there was was this endless curry—curry this, curry that—and a lot of dried-up cold meats.'

Mrs Hansen shrugged. 'I always find enough for my needs. It does not matter much.'

'What can you do? I suppose this sauce is the wrong thing for me, but you've got to take what you get when you're travelling,' said the woman. She broke off a piece of bread and passed it swiftly around her plate to scoop up what was left of the sauce. 'Starchy,' she added.

Mrs Hansen ordered a cutlet, and, after a solemn study of the menu, the other woman asked for the item listed immediately below the fish—oxtail stew. While they were waiting she ate bread and butter and shifting her mouthful comfortably from one side of her mouth to the other, accomplished a shift of her attention, too, as if her jaw and her brain had some simple mechanical connection. 'You're not from here, I suppose?' she asked, looking at Mrs Hansen with the appraisal reserved for foreigners and the licence granted by the tacit acceptance of old age on both sides.

'I have lived in the Cape, on and off, for some years,' said Mrs Hansen. 'My second husband was Danish, but settled here.'

'I could have married again. I'm not boasting, I mean, but I did have the chance, if I'd've wanted to,' said the woman. 'Somehow, I couldn't face it, after losing my first—fifty-two, that's all, and you'd have taken a lease on his life. Ah, those doctors. No wonder I feel I can't trust them a minute.'

Mrs Hansen parted the jaws of her large, elegant black bag to take out a handkerchief; the stack of letters that she always had with her—new ones arriving to take the place of old with every airmail—lay exposed. Thin letters, fat letters, big envelopes, small ones; the torn edges of foreign stamps, the large, sloping, and small, crabbed hands of foreigners writing foreign tongues. The other woman looked down upon them like a tourist, curious, impersonally insolent, envious. 'Of course, if I'd been the sort to run about a lot, I suppose it might have been different. I might have met someone really *congenial*. But there's my daughters. A mother's responsibility is never over—that's what I say. When they're little, it's little troubles. When they're grown up, it's big ones. They're all nicely married, thank God, but you know, it's always something—one of them sick, or one of the grandchildren, bless them. ... I don't suppose you've got any children. Not even from your first, I mean?'

'No,' said Mrs Hansen. 'No.' And the lie, as always, came to her as a triumph against that arrogant boy (Old Fool persisted in thinking of him as a gentle-browed youth bent over a dachshund puppy, though he was a man of forty-five by now) whom truly she had made, as she warned she would, no son of hers. When the lie was said it had the effect of leaving her breathless, as if she had just crowned a steep rise. Firmly and calmly, she leaned forward and poured herself a glass of water, as one who has deserved it.

'My, it does look fatty,' the other woman was saying over the oxtail, which had just been placed before her. 'My doctor'd have a fit if he knew I was eating this.' But eat it she did, and cutlet and roast turkey to follow. Mrs Hansen never knew whether or not her companion rounded off the meal with rhubarb pie (the woman had remarked, as she saw it carried past, that it looked soggy), because she herself had gone straight from cutlet to coffee, and, her meal finished, excused herself before the other was through the turkey course. Back in her compartment, she took off her toque at last and tied a grey chiffon scarf around her head. Then she took her red-and-gold Florentine leather cigarette case from her bag and settled down to smoke her nightly cigarette while she waited for the man to come and convert her seat into the de luxe bed Alfred had paid for in advance.

It seemed to Mrs Hansen that she did not sleep very well during the early part of the night, though she did not quite know what it was that made her restless. She was awakened, time and again, apparently by some noise that had ceased by the time she was conscious enough to identify it. The third or fourth time this happened, she woke to silence and a sense of absolute cessation, as if the world had stopped turning. But it was only the train that had stopped. Mrs Hansen lay and listened. They must be at some deserted siding in the small hours; there were no lights shining in through the shuttered window, no footsteps, no talk. The voice of a cricket, like a fingernail screeching over glass, sounded, providing, beyond the old woman's closed eyes, beyond the dark compartment and the shutters, a landscape of grass, dark, and telephone poles.

Suddenly the train gave a terrific reverberating jerk, as if it had been given a violent push. All was still again. And in the stillness, Mrs Hansen became aware of groans coming from the other side of the partition against which she lay. The groans came, bumbling and nasal, through the wood and leather; they sounded like a dog with its head buried in a cushion, worrying at the feathers. Mrs Hansen breathed out once, hard, in annoyance, and turned over; the greedy old pig, now she was suffering agonies of indigestion from that oxtail, of course. The groans continued at intervals. Once there was a muffled tinkling sound, as if a spoon had been dropped. Mrs Hansen lay tense with irritation, waiting for the train to move on and drown the woman's noise. At last, with a shake that quickly settled into a fast clip, they were off again, lickety-lack, lickety-lack, past (Mrs Hansen could imagine) the endless telephone poles, the dark grass, the black-coated cricket. Under the dialogue of the train, she was an unwilling eavesdropper to the vulgar intimacies next door; then either the groans stopped or she fell asleep in spite of them, for she heard nothing till the steward woke her with the arrival of early-morning coffee.

Mrs Hansen sponged herself, dressed, and had a quiet breakfast, undisturbed by anyone, in the dining car. The man sitting opposite her did not even ask her so much as to pass the salt. She was back in her compartment, reading, when the ticket examiner came in to take her ticket away (they would be in Johannesburg soon), and of course, she knew just where to lay her hand on it, in her bag. He leaned against the doorway while she got it out. 'Hear what happened?' he said.

'What happened?' she said uncertainly, screwing up her face because he spoke indistinctly, like most young South Africans.

'Next door,' he said. 'The lady next door, elderly lady. She died last night.'

'She died? That woman died?' She stood up and questioned him closely, as if he were irresponsible.

'Yes,' he said, checking the ticket on his list. 'The bed boy found her this morning, dead in her bed. She never answered when the steward came round with coffee, you see.'

'My God,' said Mrs Hansen. 'My God. So she died, eh?'

'Yes, lady.' He held out his hand for her ticket; he had the tale to tell all up and down the train.

With a gesture of futility, she gave it to him.

After he had gone, she sank down on the seat, beside the window, and watched the veld go by, the grasses streaming past in the sun like the long black tails of the widow birds blowing where they swung upon the fences. She had finished her paper and magazines. There was no sound but the sound of the hurrying train.

When they reached Johannesburg she had all her luggage trimly closed and ready for the porter from the hotel at which she was going to stay. She left the station with him within five minutes of the train's arrival, and was gone before the doctor, officials, and, she supposed, newspaper reporters came to see the woman taken away from the compartment next door. What could I have said to them? she thought, pleased with her sensible escape. Could I tell them she died of greed? Better not to be mixed up in it.

And then she thought of something. Newspaper reporters. No doubt there would be a piece in the Cape papers tomorrow. ELDERLY WOMAN FOUND DEAD IN CAPE–JOHANNESBURG TRAIN.

As soon as she had signed the register at the hotel she asked for a telegram form. She paused a moment, leaning on the marble-topped reception desk, looking out over the heads of the clerks. Her eyes, which were still handsome, crinkled at the corners; her nostrils lifted; her mouth, which was still so shapely because of her teeth, turned its sad corners lower in her reluctant, calculating smile. She printed Alfred's name and the address of the flat in Cape Town, and then wrote quickly, in the fine hand she had mastered more than sixty years ago: 'It was not me. Clara Hansen.'

F. Scott Fitzgerald

The Rough Crossing

I

Once on the long, covered piers, you have come into a ghostly country that is no longer Here and not yet There. Especially at night. There is a hazy yellow vault full of shouting, echoing voices. There is the rumble of trucks and the clump of trunks, the strident chatter of a crane and the first salt smell of the sea. You hurry through, even though there's time. The past, the continent, is behind you; the future is that glowing mouth in the side of the ship; this dim turbulent alley is too confusedly the present.

Up the gangplank, and the vision of the world adjusts itself, narrows. One is a citizen of a commonwealth smaller than Andorra. One is no longer so sure of anything. Curiously unmoved the men at the purser's desk, cell-like the cabin, disdainful the eyes of voyagers and their friends, solemn the officer who stands on the deserted promenade deck thinking something of his own as he stares at the crowd below. A last odd idea that one didn't really have to come, then the loud, mournful whistles, and the thing—certainly not the boat, but rather a human idea, a frame of mind—pushes forth into the big dark night.

Adrian Smith, one of the celebrities on board—not a very great celebrity, but important enough to be bathed in flash-light by a photographer who had been given his name, but wasn't sure what his subject 'did'—Adrian Smith and his blonde wife, Eva, went up to the promenade deck, passed the melancholy ship's officer, and, finding a quiet aerie, put their elbows on the rail.

'We're going!' he cried presently, and they both laughed in ecstasy. 'We've escaped. They can't get us now.'

'Who?'

He waved his hand vaguely at the civic tiara.

'All those people out there. They'll come with their posses and their warrants and list of crimes we've committed, and ring the bell at our door on Park Avenue and ask for the Adrian Smiths, but what ho! the Adrian Smiths and their children and nurse are off for France.'

'You make me think we really have committed crimes.'

'They can't have you,' he said frowning. 'That's one thing they're after me about—they know I haven't got any right to a person like you, and they're furious. That's one reason I'm glad to get away.'

'Darling,' said Eva.

She was twenty-six—five years younger than he. She was something precious to everyone who knew her.

'I like this boat better than the *Majestic* or the *Aquitania*,' she remarked, unfaithful to the ships that had served their honeymoon. 'It's much smaller.'

'But it's very slick and it has all those little shops along the corridors. And I think the staterooms are bigger.'

'The people are very formal—did you notice?—as if they thought everyone else was a card sharp. And in about four days half of them will be calling the other half by their first names.'

Four of the people came by now—a quartet of young girls abreast, making a circuit of the deck. Their eight eyes swept momentarily towards Adrian and Eva, and then swept automatically back, save for one pair which lingered for an instant with a little start. They belonged to one of the girls in the middle, who was, indeed, the only passenger of the four. She was not more than eighteen—a dark little beauty with the fine crystal gloss over her that, in brunettes, takes the place of a blonde's bright glow.

'Now, who's that?' wondered Adrian. 'I've seen her before.'

'She's pretty,' said Eva.

'Yes.' He kept wondering, and Eva deferred momentarily to his distraction; then, smiling up at him, she drew him back into their privacy.

'Tell me more,' she said.

'About what?'

'About us—what a good time we'll have, and how we'll be much better and happier, and very close always.'

'How could we be any closer?' His arm pulled her to him.

'But I mean never even quarrel any more about silly things. You know, I made up my mind when you gave me my birthday present last week'—her fingers caressed the fine seed pearls at her throat—'that I'd try never to say a mean thing to you again.'

'You never have, my precious.'

Yet even as he strained her against his side she knew that the moment of utter isolation had passed almost before it had begun. His antennæ were already out, feeling over this new world.

'Most of the people look rather awful,' he said—'little and swarthy and ugly. Americans didn't use to look like that.'

'They look dreary,' she agreed. 'Let's not get to know anybody, but just stay together.'

A gong was beating now, and stewards were shouting down the decks, 'Visitors ashore, please!' and voices rose to a strident chorus. For a while the gangplanks were thronged; then they were empty, and the jostling crowd behind the barrier waved and called unintelligible things, and kept up a grin of good will. As the stevedores began to work at the ropes a flat-faced, somewhat befuddled young man arrived in a great hurry and was assisted up the gangplank by a porter and a taxi driver. The ship having swallowed him as impassively as though he were a missionary for Beirut, a low, portentous vibration began. The pier with its faces commenced to slide by, and for a moment the boat was just a piece accidentally split off from it; then the faces became remote, voiceless, and the pier was one among many yellow blurs along the water front. Now the harbour flowed swiftly towards the sea.

On the northern parallel of latitude a hurricane was forming and moving south by southeast preceded by a strong west wind. On its course it was destined to swamp the *Peter I. Eudim* of Amsterdam, with a crew of sixty-six, to break a boom on the largest boat in the world, and to bring grief and want to the wives of several hundred seamen. This liner, leaving New York Sunday evening, would enter the zone of the storm Tuesday, and of the hurricane late Wednesday night.

II

Tuesday afternoon Adrian and Eva paid their first visit to the smoking room. This was not in accord with their intentions—they had 'never wanted to see a cocktail again' after leaving America—but they had forgotten the staccato loneliness of ships, and all activity centred about the bar. So they went in for just a minute.

It was full. There were those who had been there since luncheon, and those who would be there until dinner, not to mention a faithful few who had been there since nine this morning. It was a prosperous assembly, taking its recreation at bridge, solitaire, detective stories, alcohol, argument and love. Up to this point you could have matched it in the club or casino life of any country, but over it all played a repressed nervous energy, a barely disguised impatience that extended to old and young alike. The cruise had begun, and they had enjoyed the beginning, but the show was not varied enough to last six days, and already they wanted it to be over.

At a table near them Adrian saw the pretty girl who had stared at him on the deck the first night. Again he was fascinated by her loveliness; there was no mist upon the brilliant gloss that gleamed through the smoky confusion of the room. He and Eva had decided from the passenger list that she was probably 'Miss Elizabeth D'Amido and maid', and he had heard her called Betsy as he walked past a deck-tennis game. Among the young people with her was the flat-nosed youth who had been 'poured on board', the night of their departure; yesterday he had walked the deck morosely, but he was apparently reviving. Miss D'Amido whispered something to him, and he looked over at the Smiths with curious eyes. Adrian was new enough at being a celebrity to turn self-consciously away.

'There's a little roll. Do you feel it?' Eva demanded.

'Perhaps we'd better split a pint of champagne.'

While he gave the order a short colloquy was taking place at the other table; presently a young man rose and came over to them.

'Isn't this Mr Adrian Smith?'

'Yes.'

'We wondered if we couldn't put you down for the deck-tennis tournament. We're going to have a deck-tennis tournament.'

'Why——' Adrian hesitated.

'My name's Stacomb,' burst out the young man. 'We all know your—your plays or whatever it is, and all that—and we wondered if you wouldn't like to come over to our table.'

Somewhat overwhelmed, Adrian laughed: Mr Stacomb, glib, soft, slouching, waited; evidently under the impression that he had delivered himself of a graceful compliment.

Adrian, understanding that, too, replied: 'Thanks, but perhaps you'd better come over here.'

'We've got a bigger table.'

'But we're older and more—more settled.'

'The young man laughed kindly, as if to say, 'That's all right.'

'Put me down,' said Adrian. 'How much do I owe you?'

'One buck. Call me Stac.'

'Why?' asked Adrian, startled.

'It's shorter.'

When he had gone they smiled broadly.

'Heavens,' Eva gasped, 'I believe they are coming over.'

They were. With a great draining of glasses, calling of waiters, shuffling of chairs, three boys and two girls moving to the Smiths' table. If there was any diffidence, it was confined to the hosts; for the new additions gathered around them eagerly, eyeing Adrian with respect—too much respect—as if to say: 'This was probably a mistake and won't be amusing, but maybe we'll get something out of it to help us in our after life, like at school.'

In a moment Miss D'Amido changed seats with one of the men and placed her radiant self at Adrian's side, looking at him with manifest admiration.

'I fell in love with you the minute I saw you,' she said audibly and without self-consciousness; 'so I'll take all the blame for butting in. I've seen your play four times.'

Adrian called a waiter to take their orders.

'You see,' continued Miss D'Amido, 'we're going into a storm, and you might be prostrated the rest of the trip, so I couldn't take any chances.'

He saw that there was no undertone or innuendo in what she said, nor the need of any. The words themselves were enough, and the deference with which she neglected the young men and bent her politeness on him was somehow very touching. A little glow went over him; he was having rather more than a pleasant time.

Eva was less entertained; but the flat-nosed young man, whose name was Butterworth, knew people that she did, and that seemed to make the affair less careless and casual. She did not like meeting new people unless they had 'something to contribute', and she was often bored by the great streams of them, of all types and conditions and classes, that passed through Adrian's life. She herself 'had everything'—which is to say that she was well endowed with talents and with charm—and the mere novelty of people did not seem a sufficient reason for eternally offering everything up to them.

Half an hour later when she rose to go and see the children, she was content that the episode was over. It was colder on deck, with a damp that was almost rain, and there was a perceptible motion. Opening the door of her stateroom she was surprised to find the cabin steward sitting languidly on her bed, his head slumped upon the upright pillow. He looked at her listlessly as she came in, but made no move to get up.

'When you've finished your nap you can fetch me a new pillow-case,' she said briskly.

Still the man didn't move. She perceived then that his face was green.

'You can't be seasick in here,' she announced firmly. 'You go and lie down in your own quarters.'

'It's me side,' he said faintly. He tried to rise, gave out a little rasping sound of pain and sank back again. Eva rang for the stewardess.

A steady pitch, toss, roll had begun in earnest and she felt no sympathy for the steward, but only wanted to get him out as quick as possible. It was outrageous for a member of the crew to be seasick. When the stewardess came in Eva tried to explain this, but now her own head was whirring, and throwing herself on the bed, she covered her eyes.

'It's his fault,' she groaned when the man was assisted from the room. 'I was all right and it made me sick to look at him. I wish he'd die.'

In a few minutes Adrian came in.

'Oh, but I'm sick!' she cried.

'Why, you poor baby.' He leaned over and took her in his arms. 'Why didn't you tell me?'

'I was all right upstairs, but there was a steward—— Oh, I'm too sick to talk.'

'You'd better have dinner in bed.'

'Dinner! Oh, my heavens!'

He waited solicitously, but she wanted to hear his voice, to have it drown out the complaining sound of the beams.

'Where've you been?'

'Helping to sign up people for the tournament.'

'Will they have it if it's like this? Because if they do I'll just lose for you.'

He didn't answer; opening her eyes, she saw that he was frowning.

'I didn't know you were going in the doubles,' he said.

'Why, that's the only fun.'

'I told the D'Amido girl I'd play with her.'

'Oh.'

'I didn't think. You know I'd much rather play with you.'

'Why didn't you, then?' she asked coolly.

'It never occurred to me.'

She remembered that on their honeymoon they had been in the finals and won a prize. Years passed. But Adrian never frowned in this regretful way unless he felt a little guilty. He stumbled about, getting his dinner clothes out of the trunk, and she shut her eyes.

When a particular violent lurch startled her awake again he was dressed and tying his tie. He looked healthy and fresh, and his eyes were bright.

'Well, how about it?' he inquired. 'Can you make it, or no?'

'No.'

'Can I do anything for you before I go?'

'Where are you going?'

'Meeting those kids in the bar. Can I do anything for you?'

'No.'

'Darling, I hate to leave you like this.'

'Don't be silly. I just want to sleep.'

That solicitous frown—when she knew he was crazy to be out and away from the close cabin. She was glad when the door closed. The thing to do was to sleep, sleep.

Up—down—sideways. Hey there, not so far! Pull her round the corner there! Now roll her, right—left—— Crea-eak! Wrench! Swoop!

Some hours later Eva was dimly conscious of Adrian bending over her. She wanted him to put his arms around her and draw her up out of this dizzy lethargy, but by the time she was fully awake the cabin was empty. He had looked in and gone. When she awoke next the cabin was dark and he was in bed.

The morning was fresh and cool, and the sea was just enough calmer to make Eva think she could get up. They breakfasted in the cabin and with Adrian's help she accomplished an unsatisfactory makeshift toilet and they went up on the boat deck. The tennis tournament had already begun and was furnishing action for a dozen amateur movie cameras, but the majority of passengers were represented by lifeless bundles in deck chairs beside untasted trays.

Adrian and Miss D'Amido played their first match. She was deft and graceful; blatantly well. There was even more warmth behind her ivory skin than there had been the day before. The strolling first officer stopped and talked to her; half a dozen men whom she couldn't have known three days ago called her Betsy. She was already the pretty girl of the voyage, the cynosure of starved ship's eyes.

But after a while Eva preferred to watch the gulls in the wireless masts and the slow slide of the roll-top sky. Most of the passengers looked silly with their movie cameras that they had all rushed to get and now didn't know what to use for, but the sailors painting the lifeboat stanchions were quiet and beaten and sympathetic, and probably wished, as she did, that the voyage was over.

Butterworth sat down on the deck beside her chair.

'They're operating on one of the stewards this morning. Must be terrible in this sea.'

'Operating? What for?' she asked listlessly.

'Appendicitis. They have to operate now because we're going into worse weather. That's why they're having the ship's party tonight.'

'Oh, the poor man!' she cried, realizing that it must be her steward.

Adrian was showing off now by being very courteous and thoughtful in the game.

'Sorry. Did you hurt yourself? . . . No, it was my fault. . . . You better put on your coat right away, pardner, or you'll catch cold.'

The match was over and they had won. Flushed and hearty, he came up to Eva's chair.

'How do you feel?'

'Terrible.'

'Winners are buying a drink in the bar,' he said apologetically.

'I'm coming, too,' Eva said, but an immediate dizziness made her sink back in her chair.

'You'd better stay here. I'll send you up something.'

She felt that his public manner had hardened towards her slightly.

'You'll come back?'

'Oh, right away.'

She was alone on the boat deck, save for a solitary ship's officer who slanted obliquely as he paced the bridge. When the cocktail arrived she forced herself to drink it, and felt better. Trying to distract her mind with pleasant things, she reached back to the sanguine talks that she and Adrian had had before sailing: there was the little villa in Brittany, the children learning French—that was all she could think of now—the little villa in Brittany, the children learning French—so she repeated the words over and over to herself until they became as meaningless as the wide white sky. The why of their being here had suddenly eluded her; she felt unmotivated, accidental, and she wanted Adrian to come back quick, all responsive and tender, to reassure her. It was in the hope that there was some secret of graceful living, some real compensation for the lost, careless confidence of twenty-one, that they were going to spend a year in France.

The day passed darkly, with fewer people around and a wet sky falling. Suddenly it was five o'clock, and they were all in the bar again, and Mr Butterworth was telling her about his past. She took a good deal of champagne, but she was seasick dimly through it, as if the illness was her soul trying to struggle up through some thickening incrustation of abnormal life.

'You're my idea of a Greek goddess, physically,' Butterworth was saying.

It was pleasant to be Mr Butterworth's idea of a Greek goddess physically, but where was Adrian? He and Miss D'Amido had gone out on a forward deck to feel the spray. Eva heard herself promising to get out her colours and paint the Eiffel Tower on Butterworth's shirt front for the party to-night.

When Adrian and Betsy D'Amido, soaked with spray, opened the door with difficulty against the driving wind and came into the now-covered security of the promenade deck, they stopped and turned towards each other.

'Well?' she said. But he only stood with his back to the rail, looking at her, afraid to speak. She was silent, too, because she wanted him to be first; so for a moment nothing happened. Then she made a step towards him, and he took her in his arms and kissed her forehead.

'You're just sorry for me, that's all.' She began to cry a little. 'You're just being kind.'

'I feel terribly about it.' His voice was taut and trembling.

'Then kiss me.'

The deck was empty. He bent over her swiftly.

'No, really kiss me.'

He could not remember when anything had felt so young and fresh as her lips. The rain lay, like tears shed for him, upon the softly shining porcelain cheeks. She was all new and immaculate, and her eyes were wild.

'I love you,' she whispered. 'I can't help loving you, can I? When I first saw you—oh, not on the boat, but over a year ago—Grace Heally took me to a rehearsal and suddenly you jumped up in the second row and began telling them what to do. I wrote you a letter and tore it up.'

'We've got to go.'

She was weeping as they walked along the deck. Once more, imprudently, she held up her face to him at the door of her cabin. His blood was beating through him in wild tumult as he walked on to the bar.

He was thankful that Eva scarcely seemed to notice him or to know that he had been gone. After a moment he pretended an interest in what she was doing.

'What's that?'

'She's painting the Eiffel Tower on my shirt front for tonight,' explained Butterworth.

'There.' Eva laid away her brush and wiped her hands. 'How's that?'

'A *chef-d'œuvre*.'

Her eyes swept around the watching group, lingered casually upon Adrian.

'You're wet. Go and change.'

'You come too.'

'I want another champagne cocktail.'

'You've had enough. It's time to dress for the party.'

Unwilling she closed her paints and preceded him.

'Stacomb's got a table for nine,' he remarked as they walked along the corridor.

'The younger set,' she said with unnecessary bitterness. 'Oh, the younger set. And you just having the time of your life—with a child.'

They had a long discussion in the cabin, unpleasant on her part and evasive on his, which ended when the ship gave a sudden gigantic heave, and Eva, the edge worn off her champagne, felt ill again. There was nothing to do but to have a cocktail in the cabin, and after that they decided to go to the party—she believed him now, or she didn't care.

Adrian was ready first—he never wore fancy dress.

'I'll go on up. Don't be long.'

'Wait for me, please; it's rocking so.'

He sat down on a bed, concealing his impatience.

'You don't mind waiting, do you? I don't want to parade up there all alone.'

She was taking a tuck in an oriental costume rented from the barber.

'Ships make people feel crazy,' she said. 'I think they're awful.'

'Yes,' he muttered absently.

'When it gets very bad I pretend I'm in the top of a tree, rocking to and fro. But finally I get pretending everything, and finally I have to pretend I'm sane when I know I'm not.'

'If you get thinking that way you will go crazy.'

'Look, Adrian.' She held up the string of pearls before clasping them on. 'Aren't they lovely?'

In Adrian's impatience she seemed to move around the cabin like a figure in a slow-motion picture. After a moment he demanded:

'Are you going to be long? It's stifling in here.'

'You go on!' she fired up.

'I don't want——'

'Go on, please! You just make me nervous trying to hurry me.'

With a show of reluctance he left her. After a moment's hesitation he went down a flight to a deck below and knocked at a door.

'Betsy.'

'Just a minute.'

She came out in the corridor attired in a red pea-jacket and trousers borrowed from the elevator boy.

'Do elevator boys have fleas?' she demanded. 'I've got everything in the world on under this as a precaution.'

'I had to see you,' he said quickly.

'Careful,' she whispered. 'Mrs Worden, who's supposed to be chaperoning me, is across the way. She's sick.'

'I'm sick for you.'

They kissed suddenly, clung close together in the narrow corridor, swaying to and fro with the motion of the ship.

'Don't go away,' she murmured.

'I've got to. I've——'

Her youth seemed to flow into him, bearing him up into a delicate romantic ecstasy that transcended passion. He couldn't relinquish it; he had discovered something that he had thought was lost with his own youth forever. As he walked along the passage he knew that he had stopped thinking, no longer dared to think.

He met Eva going into the bar.

'Where've you been?' she asked with a strained smile.

'To see about the table.'

She was lovely; her cool distinction conquered the trite costume and filled him with a resurgence of approval and pride. They sat down at a table.

The gale was rising hour by hour and the mere traversing of a passage had become a rough matter. In every stateroom trunks were lashed to the washstands, and the *Vestris* disaster was being reviewed in detail by nervous ladies, tossing, ill and wretched, upon their beds. In the smoking-room a stout gentleman had been hurled backward and suffered a badly cut head; and now the lighter chairs and tables were stacked and roped against the wall.

The crowd who had donned fancy dress and were dining together had swollen to about sixteen. The only remaining qualification for membership was the ability to reach the smoking-room. They ranged from a Groton-Harvard lawyer to an ungrammatical broker they had nicknamed Gyp the Blood, but distinctions had disappeared; for the moment they were samurai, chosen from several hundred for their triumphant resistance to the storm.

The gala dinner, overhung sardonically with lanterns and streamers, was interrupted by great communal slides across the room, precipitate retirements and spilled wine, while the ship roared and complained that under the panoply of a palace it was a ship after all. Upstairs afterwards, a dozen couples tried to dance, shuffling and galloping here and there in a crazy fandango, thrust around fantastically by a will alien to their own. In view of the condition of tortured hundreds below, there grew to be something indecent about it like a revel in a house of mourning, and presently there was an egress of the ever-dwindling survivors towards the bar.

As the evening passed, Eva's feeling of unreality increased. Adrian had disappeared—presumably with Miss D'Amido—and her mind, distorted by illness and champagne, began to enlarge upon the fact; annoyance changed slowly to dark and brooding anger, grief to desperation. She had never tried to bind Adrian, never needed to—for they were serious people, with all sorts of mutual interests, and satisfied with each other—but this was a breach of the contract, this was cruel. How could he think that she didn't know?

It seemed several hours later that he leaned over her chair in the bar where she was giving some woman an impassioned lecture upon babies, and said:

'Eva, we'd better turn in.'

Her lip curled. 'So that you can leave me there and then come back to your eighteen-year——'

'Be quiet.'

'I won't come to bed.'

'Very well. Good night.'

More time passed and the people at the table changed. The stewards wanted to close up the room, and thinking of Adrian— her Adrian—off somewhere saying tender things to someone fresh and lovely, Eva began to cry.

'But he's gone to bed,' her last attendants assured her. 'We saw him go.'

She shook her head. She knew better. Adrian was lost. The long seven-year dream was broken. Probably she was punished for something she had done; as this thought occurred to her the shrieking timbers overhead began to mutter that she had guessed at last. This was for the selfishness to her mother, who hadn't wanted her to marry Adrian; for all the sins and omissions of her life. She stood up, saying she must go out and get some air.

The deck was dark and drenched with wind and rain. The ship pounded through valleys, fleeing from black mountains of water that roared towards it. Looking out at the night, Eva saw that there was no chance for them unless she could make atonement, propitiate the storm. It was Adrian's love that was demanded of her. Deliberately she unclasped her pearl necklace, lifted it to her lips—for she knew that with it went the freshest, fairest part of her life—and flung it out into the gale.

III

When Adrian awoke it was lunchtime, but he knew that some heavier sound than the bugle had called him up from his deep sleep. Then he realized that the trunk had broken loose from its lashings and was being thrown back and forth between a wardrobe and Eva's bed. With an exclamation he jumped up, but she was unharmed—still in costume and stretched out in deep sleep. When the steward had helped him secure the trunk, Eva opened a single eye.

'How are you?' he demanded, sitting on the side of her bed.

She closed the eye, opened it again.

'We're in a hurricane now,' he told her. 'The steward says it's the worst he's seen in twenty years.'

'My head,' she muttered. 'Hold my head.'

'How?'

'In front. My eyes are going out. I think I'm dying.'

'Nonsense. Do you want the doctor?'

She gave a funny little gasp that frightened him; he rang and sent the steward for the doctor.

The young doctor was pale and tired. There was a stubble of beard upon his face. He bowed curtly as he came in and, turning to Adrian, said with scant ceremony:

'What's the matter?'

'My wife doesn't feel well.'

'Well, what is it you want—a bromide?'

A little annoyed by his shortness, Adrian said: 'You'd better examine her and see what she needs.'

'She needs a bromide,' said the doctor. 'I've given orders that she is not to have any more to drink on this ship.'

'Why not?' demanded Adrian in astonishment.

'Don't you know what happened last night?'

'Why, no, I was asleep.'

'Mrs Smith wandered around the boat for an hour, not knowing what she was doing. A sailor was set to follow her, and then the medical stewardess tried to get her to bed, and your wife insulted her.'

'Oh, my heavens!' cried Eva faintly.

'The nurse and I had both been up all night with Steward Carton, who died this morning.' He picked up his case. 'I'll send down a bromide for Mrs Smith. Good-bye.'

For a few minutes there was silence in the cabin. Then Adrian put his arm around her quickly.

'Never mind,' he said. 'We'll straighten it out.'

'I remember now.' Her voice was an awed whisper. 'My pearls. I threw them overboard!'

'Threw them overboard!'

'Then I began looking for you.'

'But I was here in bed.'

'I didn't believe it; I thought you were with that girl.'

'She collapsed during dinner. I was taking a nap down here.'

Frowning, he rang the bell and asked the steward for luncheon and a bottle of beer.

'Sorry, but we can't serve any beer to your cabin, sir.'

When he went out Adrian exploded: 'This is an outrage. You were simply crazy from that storm and they can't be so high-handed. I'll see the captain.'

'Isn't that awful?' Eva murmured. 'The poor man died.'

She turned over and began to sob into her pillow. There was a knock at the door.

'Can I come in?'

The assiduous Mr Butterworth, surprisingly healthy and immaculate, came into the crazily tipping cabin.

'Well, how's the mystic?' he demanded of Eva. 'Do you remember praying to the elements in the bar last night?'

'I don't want to remember anything about last night.'

They told him about the stewardess, and with the telling the situation lightened; they all laughed together.

'I'm going to get you some beer to have with your luncheon,' Butterworth said. 'You ought to get up on deck.'

'Don't go,' Eva said. 'You look so cheerful and nice.'

'Just for ten minutes.'

When he had gone, Adrian rang for two baths.

'The thing is to put on our best clothes and walk proudly three times around the deck,' he said.

'Yes.' After a moment she added abstractedly: 'I like that young man. He was awfully nice to me last night when you'd disappeared.'

The bath steward appeared with the information that bathing was too dangerous today. They were in the midst of the wildest hurricane on the North Atlantic in ten years; there were two broken arms this morning from attempts to take baths. An elderly lady had been thrown down a staircase and was not expected to live. Furthermore, they had received the SOS signal from several boats this morning.

'Will we go to help them?'

'They're all behind us, sir, so we have to leave them to the *Mauretania*. If we tried to turn in this sea the portholes would be smashed.'

This array of calamities minimized their own troubles. Having eaten a sort of luncheon and drunk the beer provided by Butterworth, they dressed and went on deck.

Despite the fact that it was only possible to progress step by step, holding on to rope or rail, more people were abroad than on the day before. Fear had driven them from their cabins, where the trunks bumped and the waves pounded the portholes and they awaited momentarily the call to the boats. Indeed, as Adrian and Eva stood on the transverse deck above the second class, there was a bugle call, followed by a gathering of stewards and stewardesses on the deck below. But the boat was sound; it had outlasted one of its cargo—Steward James Carton was being buried at sea.

It was very British and sad. There were the rows of stiff, disciplined men and women standing in the driving rain, and there was a shape covered by the flag of the Empire that lived by the sea. The chief purser read the service, a hymn was sung, the body slid off into the hurricane. With Eva's burst of wild weeping for this humble end, some last string snapped within her. Now she really didn't care. She responded eagerly when Butterworth suggested that he get some champagne to their cabin. Her mood worried Adrian; she wasn't used to so much drinking and he wondered what he ought to do. At his suggestion that they sleep instead, she merely laughed, and the bromide the doctor had sent stood untouched on the washstand. Pretending to listen to the insipidities of several Mr Stacombs, he watched her; to his surprise and discomfort she seemed on intimate and even sentimental terms with Butterworth and he wondered if this was a form of revenge for his attention to Betsy D'Amido.

The cabin was full of smoke, the voices went on incessantly, the suspension of activity, the waiting for the storm's end, was getting on his nerves. They had been at sea only four days; it was like a year.

The two Mr Stacombs left finally, but Butterworth remained. Eva was urging him to go for another bottle of champagne.

'We've had enough,' objected Adrian. 'We ought to go to bed.'

'I won't go to bed!' she burst out. 'You must be crazy! You play around all you want, and then, when I find somebody I—I like, you want to put me to bed.'

'You're hysterical.'

'On the contrary, I've never been so sane.'

'I think you'd better leave us, Butterworth,' Adrian said. 'Eva doesn't know what she's saying.'

'He won't go. I won't let him go.' She clasped Butterworth's hand passionately. 'He's the only person that's been half decent to me.'

'You'd better go, Butterworth,' repeated Adrian.

The young man looked at him uncertainly.

'It seems to me you're being unjust to your wife,' he ventured.

'My wife isn't herself.'

'That's no reason for bullying her.'

Adrian lost his temper. 'You get out of here!' he cried.

The two men looked at each other for a moment in silence. Then Butterworth turned to Eva, said, 'I'll be back later,' and left the cabin.

'Eva, you've got to pull yourself together,' said Adrian when the door closed.

She didn't answer, looked at him from sullen, half-closed eyes.

'I'll order dinner here for us both and then we'll try to get some sleep.'

'I want to go up and send a wireless.'

'Who to?'

'Some Paris lawyer. I want a divorce.'

In spite of his annoyance, he laughed. 'Don't be silly.'

'Then I want to see the children.'

'Well, go and see them. I'll order dinner.'

He waited for her in the cabin twenty minutes. Then impatiently he opened the door across the corridor; the nurse told him that Mrs Smith had not been there.

With a sudden prescience of disaster he ran upstairs, glanced in the bar, the salons, even knocked at Butterworth's door. Then a quick round of the decks, feeling his way through the black spray and rain. A sailor stopped him at a network of ropes.

'Orders are no one goes by, sir. A wave has gone over the wireless room.'

'Have you seen a lady?'

'There was a young lady here——' He stopped and glanced around. 'Hello, she's gone.'

'She went up the stairs!' Adrian said anxiously. 'Up to the wireless room!'

The sailor ran up to the boat deck; stumbling and slipping, Adrian followed. As he cleared the protected sides of the companionway, a tremendous body struck the boat a staggering blow and, as she keeled over to an angle of forty-five degrees, he was thrown in a helpless roll down the drenched deck, to bring up dizzy and bruised against a stanchion.

'Eva!' he called. His voice was soundless in the black storm. Against the faint light of the wireless-room window he saw the sailor making his way forward.

'Eva!'

The wind blew him like a sail up against a lifeboat. Then there was another shuddering crash, and high over his head, over the very boat, he saw a gigantic, glittering white wave, and in the split second that it balanced there he became conscious of Eva, standing beside a ventilator twenty feet away. Pushing out from the stanchion, he lunged desperately towards her, just as the wave broke with a smashing roar. For a moment the rushing water was five feet deep, sweeping with enormous force towards the side, and then a human body was washed against him, and frantically he clutched it and was swept with it back towards the rail. He felt his body bump against it, but desperately he held on to his burden; then, as the ship rocked slowly back, the two of them, still joined by his fierce grip, were rolled out exhausted on the wet planks. For a moment he knew no more.

IV

Two days later, as the boat train moved tranquilly south towards Paris, Adrian tried to persuade his children to look out of the window at the Norman countryside.

'It's beautiful,' he assured them. 'All the little farms like toys. Why, in heaven's name, won't you look?'

'I like the boat better,' said Estelle.

Her parents exchanged an infanticidal glance.

'The boat is still rocking for me,' Eva said with a shiver. 'Is it for you?'

'No. Somehow, it all seems a long way off. Even the passengers looked unfamiliar going through the customs.'

'Most of them hadn't appeared above ground before.'

He hesitated. 'By the way, I cashed Butterworth's cheque for him.'

'You're a fool. You'll never see the money again.'

'He must have needed it pretty badly or he would not have come to me.'

A pale and wan girl, passing along the corridor, recognized them and put her head through the doorway.

'How do you feel?'

'Awful.'

'Me, too,' agreed Miss D'Amido. 'I'm vainly hoping my fiancé will recognize me at the Gare du Nord. Do you know two waves went over the wireless room?'

'So we heard,' Adrian answered dryly.

She passed gracefully along the corridor and out of their life.

'The real truth is that none of it happened,' said Adrian after a moment. 'It was a nightmare—an incredibly awful nightmare.'

'Then, where are my pearls?'

'Darling, there are better pearls in Paris. I'll take the responsibility for those pearls. My real belief is that you saved the boat.'

'Adrian, let's never get to know anyone else, but just stay together always—just we two.'

He tucked her arm under his and they sat close. 'Who do you suppose those Adrian Smiths on the boat were?' he demanded. 'It certainly wasn't me.'

'Nor me.'

'It was two other people,' he said, nodding to himself. 'There are so many Smiths in this world.'

G. D. H. and M. Cole

A Lesson in Crime

Joseph Newton settled himself comfortably in his corner of a first-class compartment on the Cornish Riviera express. So far, he had the compartment to himself; and if by strewing rugs, bags, books and papers about he could make himself look numerous enough to drive fellow-travellers away, there was hope he might remain undisturbed—for the long train was far from full. Let us take a look at him, and learn a little about him before his adventures begin—and end.

Age? Forty-five would not be a bad guess, though, in fact, he is rather less. As for his physical condition, 'well-nourished' is a polite description; and we, who desire to have no illusions, can safely call him paunchy, and, without positive grossness, flabby with good living. His face is puffy, and whitish under the eyes; his mouth is loose, and inclined to leer.

His fair hair, which is rapidly growing thin, is immaculately brushed, and his clothes are admirably cut and well-tended, though he has not the art of wearing them well. Altogether he looks a prosperous, thoroughly self-satisfied, and somewhat self-indulgent member of the British middle class; and that is precisely what he is.

His walk in life? You would put him down as a businessman, possibly a merchant or a middle-sized employer, not a professional man. There you would be both right and wrong. He is a professional man, in a sense; and he is certainly in business.

In fact, he is Joseph Newton, the bestseller, whose crime stories and shockers were plastered all over the bookstall he has just left with his burden of newspapers under his arm. He has sold—heaven knows how many million copies of his stories, and his serial rights, first, second, and third, cost fabulous sums to secure.

But why describe him further? All the world knows him. And now he is on his way to Cornwall, where he has a pleasant little seaside cottage with twenty-seven bedrooms.

The train starts, and Newton's carriage still remains empty save for himself. He heaves a fat sigh of relief and picks up a magazine, in which he turns instinctively to a story by himself. For the moment he cannot remember who wrote it. Poor stuff, he thinks. He must find out which 'ghost' was responsible, and sack him.

Joseph Newton was interrupted in his reflections at this point by the consciousness that someone was looking at him. He glanced up and saw the figure of a man who was standing in the corridor and staring fixedly at him, with a curious air of abstraction. Newton stared back, trying to look as unwelcoming as possible. It would be really bad luck, he felt, if someone were to invade his compartment now.

The newcomer, after a moment more of staring, pushed back the door and came in, flinging down on top of one of Newton's bags a rug and a pillow done up in a strap. He seemed to have no other luggage. Newton unwillingly got up and cleared a corner of his belongings, and the stranger sat down and began to unbuckle his strap. Then he settled himself comfortably with the pillow behind his head, and closed his eyes. 'I hope to goodness he doesn't snore,' Newton thought.

While our second traveller is thus peacefully settling himself for a doze, we may as well take a good look at him also; for it may be important to know him later on. He is a scraggy little man, probably of sixty or more, with a completely bald pink head and a straggling grey beard which emerges from an incredibly folded and puckered yellow chin. His height is hardly more than five foot six, and his proportions are puny; but there is a wiriness about his spare person that contrasts strongly with Newton's fleshy bulk.

He is dressed, not so much ill as with a carelessness amounting to eccentricity. His clothes, certainly cut by a good tailor, hang in bags all over him. His pockets bulge. His waistcoat is buttoned up wrong, and sets awry, and his shirt has come apart at the neck, so that a disconsolate shirt-stud is hanging out on one side, while his red tie is leaning towards the other. Moreover the sole of one of his boots has come loose, and flaps helplessly as his crossed legs swing slowly to the rhythm of the train.

Yet, despite these appearances, the newcomer is certainly a gentleman, and one is inclined to deem him eccentric rather than poor. He might be an exceptionally absent-minded professor; though, as a matter of fact, he is not. But who he is Joseph Newton has no idea.

For some time there was silence in the compartment, as the Cornish Riviera sped westward past the long spreading ribbon of London. Newton's fellow-traveller did not snore. His eyes were closed whenever Newton glanced at him; and yet between whiles the novelist had still a queer feeling of being stared at. He told himself it was nonsense, and tried to bury himself in a Wild West story; but the sensation remained with him. Suddenly, as the train passed Maidenhead Station, his companion spoke, in a quiet positive voice, as of one used to telling idiots what idiots they were. A professorial voice, with a touch of Scots accent.

'Talking of murders,' it said, 'you have really no right to be so careless.'

'Eh?' said Newton, so startled that his magazine dropped from his hand to the floor. 'Eh, what's that?'

'I said you had no right to be so careless,' repeated the other.

Newton retrieved his magazine, and looked his fellow-traveller contemptuously up and down. 'I am not aware,' he said, 'that we were talking of murders, or of anything else, for that matter.'

'There, you see,' said the other, 'you did hear what I said the first time. What I mean to say is that, if you expect intelligent people to read your stories, you might at least trouble to make them plausible.'

Newton suppressed the rejoinder that rose instantly to his lips. It was that he had far too large a circulation among fools to bother about what intelligent people thought. He only said, 'I doubt, sir, if you are likely to find my conversation any more satisfactory than my books,' and resumed his magazine.

'Probably not,' said the stranger. 'I expect success has spoiled you. But you had some brains to begin with.... Those Indian stories of yours——'

Perhaps no other phrase would have induced Joseph Newton to embark upon a conversation with the stranger. But nobody nowadays ever read or bothered about his Indian stories, though he was very well aware that they were the best things he had ever done.

'——had glimmerings of quality,' the other was saying, 'and you might have accomplished something had you not taken to writing for money.'

'Are you aware, sir,' Newton said, 'that you are being excessively rude?'

'Quite,' said the other with calm satisfaction. 'I always am. It is so good for people. And really, in your last book, you have exceeded the limit.'

'Which of my last books are you talking about?' asked Newton, hovering between annoyance and amusement.

'It is called *The Big Noise*,' said the other, sighing softly.

'Oh, that,' said Newton.

'Now, in that book,' the stranger went on, 'you call the heroine Elinor and Gertrude on different pages. You cannot make up your mind whether her name was Robbins with two *b*'s or with one. You have killed the corpse in one place on Sunday and in another on Monday evening. That corpse was discovered twelve hours after the murder still wallowing in a pool of wet blood. The coroner committed no fewer than seventeen irregularities in conducting the inquest; and, finally, you have introduced three gangs, a mysterious Chinaman, an unknown poison that leaves no trace, and a secret society of international Jews high up in the political world.'

The little old man held up his hands in horror as he ended the grisly recital.

'Well,' Newton asked, 'any more?'

'Alas, yes,' said the other. 'The volume includes, besides many misprints, fifteen glaring inconsistencies, nine cases of gross ignorance, and enough grammatical mistakes to—to stretch from Paddington to Penzance.'

This time Newton laughed outright. 'You seem to be a very earnest student of my writings,' he said.

The stranger picked up the rug from his knees and folded it neatly beside him. He removed the pillow, and laid that down too. He then moved across to the corner opposite Newton and, taking a jewelled cigarette case from his pocket, selected a cigarette, returned the case to his pocket, found a match, lighted up, and began to smoke. Then he again drew out the case and offered it to Newton. 'Lavery's,' he said. 'I know your favourite brand.'

As a matter of fact, Newton never smoked Lavery's; but for a handsome sum he allowed his face, and a glowing testimonial to their virtues, to appear on their advertisements. Well, he might as well find out what the things were like. He took the proffered cigarette, and the stranger obligingly gave him a light. Newton puffed. Yes, they were good stuff—better than might be expected, though rather heavy.

'Now, in my view,' the stranger was saying, 'the essence of a really good murder is simplicity. All your books—all most people's books—have far too much paraphernalia about them. A really competent murderer would need no special appliances, and practically no preparations. Ergo, he would be in far less danger of leaving any clues behind him. Why, oh why, Mr Newton, do you not write a murder story on those lines?'

Again Newton laughed. He was disposed to humour the old gentleman. 'It wouldn't make much of a story,' he said, 'if the murderer really left no clues.'

'Oh, but there you are wrong,' said the other. 'What is needed is a perfectly simple murder, followed by a perfectly simple solution—so simple that only a great mind could think of it, by penetrating to the utter simplicity of the mind of the murderer.'

'I can't abide those psychological detectives,' Newton said. 'You'd better go and read Mr Van Dine.' ('Or some of those fellows who would give their ears for a tenth of my sales,' his expression added.)

'Dear me, you quite misunderstood me. That wasn't what I meant at all. There would be no psychology in the story I have in mind. It would be more like William Blake's poetry.'

'Mad, you mean,' said Newton.

'Crystal sane,' replied the other. 'Perhaps it will help you if I illustrate my point. Shall I outline the sort of murder I have in mind?'

'If you like,' said Newton, who found himself growing suddenly very sleepy.

'Very well,' said the stranger. 'Then I'll just draw down the blinds.'

He jumped up and lowered the blinds on the corridor side of the compartment.

'That's better,' he said. 'Now we shall be undisturbed. Now supposing—only supposing, of course—that there were two men in a railway carriage just like us, and they were perfect strangers, but one of them did not really care for the other's face—— Are you listening, Mr Newton?'

'Yes,' said Newton, very sleepily. He was now having real difficulty in keeping his eyes open.

'And further, supposing neither of them had brought any special paraphernalia with him, except what any innocent traveller might be carrying—say, a rug, a pillow, and a rug-strap——'

As he spoke, the stranger picked up the rug-strap from the seat beside him.

'Hey, what's that about a rug-strap?' said Newton, roused for a moment by a connection of ideas he was too sleepy to sort out.

'Except, of course, just one doped cigarette, containing an opiate—strong, but in no wise fatal,' the other went on blandly.

'What the——?' murmured Newton, struggling now vainly against an absolutely stupefying drowsiness.

'There would really be nothing to prevent him from committing a nice, neat murder, would there?' the old man continued, rising as he spoke with startling agility and flinging the loop of the rug-strap over Newton's head. 'Now, would there?' he repeated, as he drew it tight around his victim's neck, and neatly fastened it. Newton's mouth came wide open; his tongue protruded, and he began to gurgle horribly; his eyes stuck out from his head.

'And then,' said the stranger, 'the pillow would come in so handy to finish him off.' He dragged Newton down on the seat, placed the pillow firmly on his upturned face, and sat on it, smiling delightedly. The gurgling slowly ceased.

'The rug,' the cheerful voice went on, 'has proved to be super-fluous. Really, Mr Newton, murder is even easier than I supposed—though it is not often, I imagine, that a lucky chance enables one to do a service to the literary craft at the same time.'

Newton said nothing; for he was dead.

The stranger retained his position a little longer, still smiling gently to himself. Then he rose, removed the pillow from Newton's face, and, after a careful survey of the body, undid the strap. Next, he picked up a half-smoked cigarette and threw it out of the window, folded his rug neatly, did it and the pillow up in the strap, and, opening the door into the corridor, walked quietly away down the train.

'What a pity!' he murmured to himself as he went. 'It would make such a good story; and I am afraid the poor fellow will never have the sense to write it.'

The body of Joseph Newton was actually discovered by a restaurant car attendant who was going round to collect orders for the first lunch. Opening the door of a first-class compartment, which had all its blinds drawn down, he found Newton, no pleasant sight and indubitably dead, stretched out upon the seat where his companion had left him.

Without waiting to do more than make sure the man was dead, he scuttled along to fetch the guard. A brief colloquy of train-officials then took place in the fatal compartment, and it was decided to stop the train short of Newbury Station, and send for the police before anyone had a chance of leaving it. It seemed clear, as there had been no stop since they left Paddington, that the murderer must still be on it, unless he had leaped from an express travelling at full speed.

The police duly arrived, inspected the body, hunted the compartment in vain for traces of another passenger—for the murderer had taken the precaution of wearing gloves throughout his demonstration—took the name and address of every person on the train, to the number of some hundreds, had the carriage in which the murder had occurred detached, with much shunting and grunting, from the rest of the train, and finally allowed the delayed express to proceed.

Only those travellers who had been actually in the coach of which Newton's compartment had formed a part were kept back for further inquiries. But Newton's companion was not among them. Having given his correct name and address to the police, he proceeded quietly upon his journey in the empty first-class compartment two coaches farther back to which he had moved after his successful experiment in simplicity.

There were four hundred and ninety-eight passengers on the Cornish Riviera express whose names were taken by the police at Newbury; or, if you count Newton, four hundred and ninety-nine. Add guards and attendants, restaurant-car staff, and the occupants of a travelling Post Office van—total five hundred and nineteen.

Of these one hundred and twenty-six were women, one hundred and fifty-three children, and the rest men. That allowed for quite enough possible suspects for the police to follow up. They were followed up, exhaustively. But it did not appear that any single person among them had any acquaintance with Joseph Newton, or any connection with him save as readers of his books. Nor did a meticulous examination of Newton's past suggest the shadow of a reason why he should have been murdered.

The police tried their hardest, and the public and the Press did their best to assist, for the murder of a bestseller, by a criminal who left no clue, was enough to excite anybody's imagination. Several individuals, in their enthusiasm, went so far as to confess to the crime, and gave Scotland Yard several days' work in disproving their statements. But nothing helpful was forthcoming, and at long last the excitement died down.

It was more than three months later that the young Marquis of Queensferry called upon Henry Wilson, formerly the chief official of Scotland Yard, and now the foremost private detective in England. His modest request was that Wilson should solve for him the mystery of Joseph Newton's murder.

When Wilson asked him why he wanted it solved, the Marquis explained that it was for a bet. It appeared that his old uncle, the

Honourable Roderick Dominic Acres-Noel, had bet him fifty thousand pounds to a penny he could not solve the problem, and he, who had the title but not the money, would be very willing to lay his hands on fifty thousand pounds which his uncle, who had the money but not the title, would never miss. Asked the reason for so unusual a bet, he replied that the reason was Uncle Roderick, who was always betting on something, the sillier the better.

'Our family's like that, you know,' the Marquis added. 'We're all mad. And my uncle was quite excited about the case, because he was on the train when it happened. He even wrote to *The Times* about it.'

Wilson rejected the idea that he could solve a case which had utterly baffled Scotland Yard when the trail was fresh, now that it was stone cold, and all clues, presumably, vanished into limbo. Even the most lavish promises of shares in the fifty thousand pounds did not tempt him, and he sent the young Marquis away with a flea in his ear.

But, after the Marquis had gone, he found that he could not get the case out of his head. In common with everybody else, he had puzzled his brains over it at the time; but it was weeks since he had given it a thought. But now—here it was again—bothering his mind.

Hang it all, it wasn't reasonable—it was against nature—that a man should be able to murder another man and get away without leaving any clue at all. So, at any rate, the Marquis's crazy old uncle seemed to think, unless, indeed, he was merely crazy. Most likely he was.

Wilson could not say exactly at what moment he decided to have one more shot at this impossible mystery. Perhaps it was when he recollected that, according to the Marquis, Mr Acres-Noel had himself travelled on that train to Cornwall. It might be that Mr Acres-Noel had noticed something that the police had missed; he was just the sort of old gentleman who would enjoy keeping a tit-bit of information to himself. At any rate, it was one thing one could try.

Wilson rang up his old colleague, Inspector Blaikie, at Scotland Yard, and Blaikie guffawed at him.

'Solve it, by all means,' he said. 'We'll be delighted. We're sick of the sound of Newton's name. . . . Yes, old Acres-Noel was on the train—I don't know anything more about him. . . . Oh, mad as a hatter. Completely . . . Yes, he wrote to *The Times*, and they printed it. . . . Three days afterwards, I think. Shall I have it looked up

for you? . . . Right you are. Let us know when you catch the murderer, won't you?'

Wilson sent for his own file of *The Times*, and looked up the letter
of Mr Acres-Noel. *The Times* had not thought it worth the honour
of the middle page, but fortunately had not degraded it into the
'Points' column.

'Sir,' it ran,

'The methods of the police in dealing with the so-called Newton
Mystery appear to show more than the usual official incompetence.
As one of the passengers on the train on which Mr Newton died,
I have been subjected to considerable annoyance—and I may add
compensated in part by some amusement—at the fruitless and irre-
levant inquiries made by the police.

'It is plain the police have no notion of the motives which promp-
ted the murder. Their inquiries show that. If they would devote
more attention to *thinking* what the motive was, and less to the ac-
cumulation of useless information, the apparent complexity of the
case would disappear. The truth is usually simple—too simple for
idiots to see. *Why* was Newton murdered? Answer that, and it will
appear plainly that only one person could have murdered him.
Motive is essentially individual.

'I am, yours, etc.,

'R. D. Acres-Noel.'

'Upon my word,' said Wilson to himself, 'that's a very odd letter.'

He read it several times over, staring at it as if the name of the
murderer was written between the lines.

Suddenly he leaped to his feet, and with an excitement he seldom
showed, dashed down Whitehall to Inspector Blaikie's office.
Within ten minutes he was making a proposition to that official
which left him starkly incredulous.

'I know,' Wilson persisted, 'it isn't a certainty, it's a thousand
to one chance. But it *is* a chance, and I want to try it. I'm not
asking the Department to commit itself in any way, only to let me
have a couple of men standing by. Don't you see, the whole point
about this extraordinary letter is the way it stresses the question of
motive? And, more than that, it suggests that the writer knows
what the motive was. Now, how could he do that unless——'

'But, if that's so, the man's mad!' Blaikie protested. 'Whoever
heard of anybody murdering a complete stranger just to *show*
him?'

'Well, he certainly is mad, isn't he? You said so yourself, and his family's notoriously crazy.'

'He'll have to be pretty well off his rocker,' Blaikie remarked, 'if he's to be kind enough to come and shove his neck in a noose for you.'

'One can but try,' Wilson said. 'If you won't help me I'm going to try alone. I must have one shot at getting to the bottom of it.' And eventually Blaikie agreed.

The upshot was that Wilson, immediately after his interview, arranged for the posting of the following letter, forged with extreme care so as to imitate the handwriting of the supposed author. It was dispatched from the pillar-box nearest to Joseph Newton's Cornish cottage.

'Dear Mr Acres-Noel,' it said,

'Ever since our chance meeting a few months ago, I have been thinking over the very interesting demonstration you were kind enough to give me on that occasion. May I confess, however, that I am still not quite satisfied; and I should be even more deeply obliged if I could induce you to repeat it. As it happens, I shall be returning to London this week-end, and travelling down again to Cornwall on the Riviera express next Wednesday. If you too should chance to be travelling that way, perhaps we may meet again.

'Yours very truly,

'Joseph Newton.'

Someone remarkably like the late Joseph Newton settled himself comfortably in the corner of a first-class compartment in the Cornish Riviera express. He had the compartment to himself, and, although the train had begun to fill up, no other traveller had entered when the train drew out of the station. Very discreetly, passengers who came near it had been warned away by the station officials.

The train had not yet gathered its full speed when the solitary traveller became conscious that someone was standing outside the compartment and staring in at him. He raised his eyes from the magazine he was reading and looked back. Slowly the newcomer pushed back the sliding door, entered the compartment, and sat down in the far corner.

He was a little old man, with a straggling beard, wearing very shabby clothes. He flung down on the seat beside him a rug and a pillow tied up in a strap. Undoing his bundle, he settled himself with the pillow behind his head, the rug over his knees, and the strap on the seat beside him. Then he closed his eyes.

Wilson did and said nothing. It was nervous work, waiting for his cue. But by this time he knew he was right. The millionth chance had come off.

The train flashed at length—it seemed hours—through Maidenhead Station. Suddenly the old man spoke.

'Talking of murders,' he said, 'it is my turn to apologise. I am afraid I bungled it last time.'

'Not at all,' said Wilson, hoping that his voice would not give him away; 'but if you would kindly just show me again how——'

'With pleasure,' said the old man.

He moved with alacrity to the corner opposite Wilson, took from his pocket a jewelled cigarette case, and proffered it. Wilson took a cigarette, and did a second's rapid thinking before the match was produced. A cigarette was something he had not allowed for, and it might even turn out to be poisoned. However, no use to hesitate now. He suffered Mr Acres-Noel to light it, and the heavy sweetish taste confirmed his fears.

Fortunately, however, it was hardly alight before the other rose and went to the window.

'You won't mind my pulling down the blinds, will you?' he said; and Wilson took advantage of his movement to effect a lightning exchange of the suspicious cigarette for one of his own. This was a relief, but clearly he must show some signs of being affected by it. Sleepiness seemed the most likely cue. He yawned.

'You follow me so far, I trust,' said the other.

'Perfectly,' said Wilson slowly. 'Please—go——' Slowly his eyes closed, and his head began to wag.

The old man seized the rug-strap.

'This is the next step,' he said, attempting to cast it over Wilson's head. But Wilson sprang to his feet, warded off the strap, and pressed a button beside him which had been fixed to communicate with the adjoining compartment.

Almost as he grappled with his now frenzied antagonist, two stalwart policemen in plain clothes rushed in to his aid. Mr Acres-Noel, alternately protesting his innocence and shrieking with wild laughter, was soon safely secured. The train slowed down and stopped at the deserted station of Newbury Racecourse, where captors and captive descended almost unnoticed. Then it sped upon its way.

Mr Acres-Noel, safe in Broadmoor, has only one complaint. The authorities will not supply him with Joseph Newton's new books. He wants to see whether that popular writer has benefited by his lesson in practical criminology.

Acknowledgements

The editor wishes to thank the authors (or their agents or trustees) and publishers who have granted permission to reproduce the following copyright material:

'An Elaborate Elopement' by W. W. Jacobs. Reprinted by permission of the Society of Authors as the literary representative of the Estate of the late W. W. Jacobs.

'The Better Part of Valour' by Celia Dale from *Winter's Tales* No *21* (Macmillan). Reprinted by permission of Curtis Brown.

'The Long-Distance Train' by W. B. Maxwell, from *Great English Short Stories* (Harrap).

'Miss Winchelsea's Heart' from *Complete Short Stories* by H. G. Wells (Ernest Benn). Reprinted by permission of the Estate of the late H. G. Wells.

'Enemies' from *Selected Stories* by Nadine Gordimer (Jonathan Cape). © 1975 by the author. Reprinted by permission of Viking Press Inc.

'The Rough Crossing' by F. Scott Fitzgerald, from *The Bodley Head Scott Fitzgerald* by permission of The Bodley Head. Also from *The Stories of F. Scott Fitzgerald*, selected by Malcolm Cowley, by permission of Charles Scribner's Sons. © 1951 by Charles Scribner's Sons. © 1929 by the Curtis Publishing Co. © renewed 1957 by The Curtis Publishing Co. and Frances Scott Fitzgerald Lanahan.

'A Lesson in Crime' by G. D. H. and M. Cole. Reprinted by permission of the Estate of the late G. D. H. Cole.

S